The kiss

He'd made no attempt to do more than just kiss her, yet she'd felt as if every part of her body was under siege.

"Why?" she managed to ask, and saw Nikos's lips curve ironically.

"Because I wanted to."

"Do you always do exactly as you want?" she countered.

"Not always, but you have a mouth made for kissing…"

KAY THORPE was born in Sheffield, U.K. She tried out a variety of jobs after leaving school. Writing began as a hobby, becoming a way of life only after she had her first completed novel accepted for publication in 1968. Since then, she's written over fifty novels and lives now with her husband, son, German shepherd dog and lucky black cat on the outskirts of Chesterfield in Derbyshire. Her interests include reading, hiking and travel.

Look out for Kay's next book in Harlequin Presents®: *The Italian Match*, #2312, on sale in March.

The Thirty-Day Seduction

KAY THORPE

ISLAND ROMANCES

TORONTO • NEW YORK • LONDON
AMSTERDAM • PARIS • SYDNEY • HAMBURG
STOCKHOLM • ATHENS • TOKYO • MILAN • MADRID
PRAGUE • WARSAW • BUDAPEST • AUCKLAND

ISBN 0-373-80528-4

THE THIRTY-DAY SEDUCTION

First North American Publication 2002.

Copyright © 1998 by Kay Thorpe.

Visit us at www.eHarlequin.com

Printed in U.S.A.

CHAPTER ONE

STEADYING herself as the boat rode the spreading bow wave from a passing tourist carrier, Chelsea viewed the island ahead with anticipation tempered by a certain disquiet. Ethics at war with ambition again, she acknowledged wryly; the bane of her professional life at times. Given the same opportunity, how many in her line would hesitate to take advantage?

"Skalos," declared the man at the wheel of the luxurious cabin cruiser, reducing speed. "Welcome to my home."

Chelsea turned her head to smile at the handsome young Greek, admiring the lithe lines of his olive-skinned body, clad only in denim shorts at present.

"I hope your family feel the same way."

White teeth sparkled in the sunlight. "My friends are always welcomed!"

"Even foreign ones?"

He laughed. "We have no quarrel with the English."

"All the same," she murmured, "we're not exactly *old* friends."

"We're neither of us old enough to be *old* friends," he returned equably. "And why should it make a difference how long we've known each other? Two days or two years; it would be the same. We are—how do you say it—comparable?"

"Compatible." Which they certainly appeared to be, Chelsea reflected. From the first moment of meeting, back there in Skiathos, they had got on like the prover-

5

bial house on fire. All the same, it was doubtful if she would be doing this had Dion not been who he was.

"How many Pandrossoses live on the island altogether?" she asked casually as the low-hilled, wooded landscape took on detail in the hot afternoon sunlight.

"Nikos is the only one, apart from ourselves," Dion confirmed. "But there are several other families allowed to make their homes there too."

"It's privately owned?"

"Owned by the company." The handsome features darkened for a moment. "The company my father should have been made president of four years ago when his brother died."

From what she knew of Pandrossos affairs, the deceased president's son, Nikos Pandrossos, had inherited too much power in the way of company shares to be ousted by his uncle, Chelsea mused. Nor could he be faulted in his handling of the business since. Pandrossos Shipping had gone from strength to strength.

He would be thirty-six now, which was young still to be in such a position. A multi-millionaire, it went without saying. Three years ago his wife and mother had both been drowned in a boating accident, leaving him with a young son. That was all the personal detail anyone appeared to know of the man. An enigma, that was Nikos Pandrossos. As stirring a challenge to any self-respecting journalist as a red rag to a bull.

Coming into an inheritance at eighteen from her maternal grandfather, sufficient to keep her in a reasonable degree of comfort, Chelsea had seen no reason to opt out of university, emerging three years later with a first-class degree and an overriding desire to become something big in the world of journalism. She'd been lucky enough to land a job on a leading newspaper, which had supplied the grounding she needed, and moved on from there to *World Magazine* for a year, during which she had made something of a name for herself. With no financial pressures, she'd been able to go freelance after that, enjoying the freedom of being able to choose her own storylines, most of which she had found little difficulty in selling. At twenty-five she had what most people—including herself—would consider an enviable lifestyle.

Her decision to take a couple of months out, flitting around the Greek Islands, had elicited no more than a resigned injunction to take care from her parents, who had long ago learned to accept her independence. Skiathos had been her third port of call, after Limnos and Alonissos, with the intention of fitting in as many points south as she could manage over the coming weeks. Something she had always wanted to do, and from which she hoped to gain enough material for a whole series of articles.

She had been sitting over morning coffee at one of the harbour tavernas, watching the boats coming and going, when Dion had arrived, drawing every female eye in the vicinity as he leapt ashore after securing his craft. A young man well accustomed to having his pick, Chelsea had judged, as he'd stood, hands thrust into the pockets of his tight-fitting designer jeans, viewing the immediate prospects. She'd looked away before the discerning dark eyes found her, but she'd sensed his gaze coming to rest on her.

He hadn't been the first Greek male to find her combination of long wheat-gold hair and vivid blue eyes an instant attraction by any means. She had formulated a nice line in cool, composed rejection of all take-over bids, which had stood her in pretty good stead up until then. Dion, however, was made of sterner stuff. Instead of moving on, he'd laughed and taken a seat, introducing himself with a charm calculated to melt the most resistant of hearts.

The name alone had been enough to dry any protest she might have made, the discovery by dint of carefully casual questioning that he was indeed a relative of the man so many had tried and failed to interview a potent force.

Even so, if she hadn't liked Dion as a person that would have been it, Chelsea assured herself now. She'd enjoyed every minute of the time they'd spent together—especially after Dion had proved himself unexpectedly willing to accept their relationship on her terms. His announcement that he had to return home in order to attend his young cousin's fifth birthday celebrations, and his invitation to accompany him, had elicited mixed feelings, but the enticement had proved too strong in the end. This would be the closest anyone from her part of the world had ever managed to get to Nikos Pandrossos the man. If she could manage to talk him into granting her an interview, it would be a real feather in her journalistic cap.

They were coming into a small bay where a graceful twin-masted yacht already rode at anchor. Trees backed the curve of sand, giving way to one side to reveal what looked like the start of a narrow roadway—if the car parked there was anything to go by. A man alighted from the vehicle as Dion cut the engine to bring the launch in to a well-timed stop at the jetty built out from a rocky platform, lifting a hand in brief greeting.

"Cousin Nikos," said Dion. "He must have just got in himself."

Chelsea made no reply, aware of her suddenly increased pulse-rate as she studied the waiting figure. Taller than the average Greek, with shoulders like an ox beneath the tautly stretched white T-shirt, he looked intimidating even from this distance. He was wearing jeans, close-fitting about lean hips and outlining the muscular strength of his thighs. Masculine as they came—and dangerous with it, came the mental rider.

Dion leapt out and tied up the boat before extending a hand to assist her onto the jetty.

"I'll take your bag," he said, reaching for the holdall that was the only luggage she had allowed herself this trip. His eyes sparkled devilishly at her involuntary protest. "Must I fight with you for it?"

Laughing, Chelsea gave way. "I suppose I'm too used to doing things for myself," she said, falling into step at his side along the jetty.

The laughter faded as they descended the carved steps from the rocky platform and trod the stretch of sand to where Nikos Pandrossos awaited their coming. Dark as Dion's, his eyes scanned her from the toes upwards with a thoroughness that brought faint flags of colour into her cheeks, taking in the shapely length of leg revealed by the brief white shorts, the curve of hip and slender waist-line—lingering for a deliberate moment on the firm thrust of her breasts beneath the halter-necked top—before lifting to meet her blue regard with a faint but unmistakable curl of a lip.

"This is Chelsea Lovatt, Nikos," declared Dion, sounding just a mite confrontational to Chelsea's ears. "An English friend come to spend a few days."

"Chelsea?" queried the older man, not having shifted his stance. "You're named after a district of London?"

"I'm named after a character in a book my mother read while she was carrying me," Chelsea answered lightly, gathering her wits. "I think she hoped I might turn out the same."

The curl increased a fraction. "And did you?"

"I've no idea," she parried. "I never read the book." She put out a hand, registering the surprise that sprang momentarily in his eyes. "I'm honoured to meet you, Kirie Pandrossos."

The dark head inclined, revealing the merest hint of grey at the temples as a shaft of sunlight touched the thickly curling pelt of his hair. His hand was cool to the touch, fingers closing over hers in a grasp of tempered steel, sending a thrill like an electric shock the length of her arm.

"The honour is all mine, *despinis,*" he mocked.

Chelsea resisted the urge to snatch her hand away the moment he released it, feeling the tingle still in her fingers as she thrust them into the pocket of her shorts. Having met the man, she was beginning to realise just how formidable a task she had set herself. She was here under false pretences to start with, which was hardly going to help her case. There was every likelihood that he would have her deported—from the island, at least— the moment he discovered her real purpose.

Never say die, she told herself firmly, refusing to give way. Challenge was her lifeblood.

"Will you give us a lift to the house?" asked Dion.

"I'd scarcely leave you to await other transport," returned his cousin. He turned to open the Range Rover's front passenger door, noting Chelsea's involuntary hesitation with a sardonic little smile. "I don't bite. Not unless I'm provoked. If you'd feel more comfortable in the rear, however..."

"I'm happy to sit anywhere," she said airily, mentally girding her loins again. "Thank you, *kirie.*"

"You may call me Nikos," he declared as she slid into the seat.

"Thank you, Nikos, then." Chelsea took care to erad-icate any hint of irony from her tone. "I'm not much for formality either."

Dark eyes dwelt for a meaningful moment on the long stretch of lightly tanned leg, even further revealed by the pull on her shorts. "So it may be assumed."

He closed the door before she could come up with a response, leaving her feeling more than a little over-exposed. Dion had donned his shirt again before leaving the boat, but had given her no reason to believe herself inadequately dressed. Considering the scanty wardrobe she had with her, she was probably going to have a problem meeting the criteria anyway, she reflected rue-fully. The things she'd packed had been chosen for their lightness of weight and washability rather than propriety.

Dion got into the rear seat, leaving his cousin to go around and slide behind the wheel. The car was turned about in three short, sharp moves and headed up the curving incline between the trees. Acutely aware of the muscular thigh she could see on the periphery of her vision, Chelsea turned her attention to the view from the side window as they breasted the final rise and emerged from the tree line.

From here she was looking directly towards the main-land, some five or six miles distant, the mountainous horizon line hazed by heat. Close by lay another, very much smaller island, bearing what looked like the crum-bling remains of a small tower on its highest point.

"Does the ruin over there have any significance?" she asked with interest, anticipating some historic prove-nance.

"It's just a ruin," said Dion.

"All that's left of what was once a tiny chapel," expounded his cousin. "We've never taken the trouble to explore its origins, but you're at liberty to do so, should you wish it."

Chelsea gave him a swift glance, struck by the strength of the carved profile with its high-bridged nose and clean jawline. His mouth was well-shaped, lips firm. Wonderful to kiss, came the unwonted thought, hastily discarded.

"That's very kind of you," she said, "but I'm hardly going to be here long enough to start looking into historical detail."

"You have other commitments?"

"Well, no. At least, nothing concrete. I'm just going where the fancy takes me for the next few weeks—seeing as much of the islands as I can."

"Alone?" The tone left little doubt of his opinion. "Is that wise?"

"I can take care of myself," she returned without undue emphasis. "And travelling alone means I only have myself to please."

"You have family back home?"

"Parents, yes."

"They saw no harm in allowing you to do this?"

Her laugh was just a little short. "They have every confidence in me."

"But obviously little authority over you."

"In my country, women my age are considered old enough to govern their own lives."

"In *my* country, women your age are normally answerable to their husbands," came the unmoved response. "Is there no man in your life?"

"No one I plan on marrying, if that's what you

mean." Chelsea was fast losing patience with this inquisition. "I've no interest whatsoever in marriage."

Nikos gave her another of those swift, assessing
glances. "You should think seriously about it while you
still have the time."

About to let fly with a pithy answer, Chelsea caught
herself up. Considering the reason she was here at all,
she was hardly doing her case much good by getting
ratty with the man. She needed to cultivate him, not
antagonise him. What she didn't need at the moment was
to let drop any hint of her true colours.

"I appreciate your concern for my welfare, *kirie,* really I do," she said on a lighter note. "Few would take
the trouble."

The overture made no visible impression. "You were
to call me Nikos," was all he said.

Quiet up until now in the back, Dion obviously decided it was time he made his presence felt. "My sister
will be happy to have you here," he said. "She's always
complaining of the shortage of feminine companionship.
Florina is unmarried too—although she hopes to be wed
before *too* much more time passes." The last with an
odd emphasis. "You'll like each other, I'm sure."

Chelsea hoped he was right. Being here under false
pretences was bad enough, without finding herself at
odds with any member of his family. Abandoning the
whole idea would probably be the wisest course, but she
couldn't bring herself to do it. Not while there was any
chance at all of achieving her aim. Nikos would be a
hard nut to crack, but she might just manage it if she
put her mind to it. First and foremost, she had to get
beneath that guard of his.

"If she speaks English as fluently as the two of you

do there'll certainly be no problem in communicating,"
she said. "My Greek is pretty basic as yet."

"Travel broadens the vocabulary," said Nikos. "As
does tourism also."

Chelsea's brows drew together. "You're involved in
the tourist industry?"

"The whole of Greece is involved in the tourist industry," came the dry return. "Our economy, to a great
extent, depends upon it."

"I shouldn't have thought you met all that many tour-
ists yourself, though," she ventured, unable to visualise
this man mingling with the average package dealers.
"The island being private, I mean."

"Our lives are hardly confined to Skalos," he said,
making her feel a bit of an idiot.

"Does Dimitris know yet that he's to have a birthday
party?" asked Dion, before she could make any further
comment. "Or is it still to be a surprise?"

"Better he should be surprised rather than disap-
pointed should anything go amiss," his cousin replied.
"Do you like children?" he added to Chelsea.

"I couldn't eat a whole one," she quipped before she
could stop herself, drawing a splutter of laughter from
the rear. "Sorry, that was crass," she apologised, neither
daring nor caring to glance in Nikos's direction. She
added cautiously, "I like *some* children."

"You'll love Dimitris," Dion assured her. "He's a
real little character!"

"You're welcome to attend the party if you wish,"
invited his cousin, leaving Chelsea feeling that the
younger man hadn't left him much choice.

An opportunity to see the Pandrossos homestead was
hardly to be turned down, however, though it seemed
necessary to at least make the gesture.

"That's very kind of you, she said formally, "but I wouldn't want to intrude on a family occasion."

Nikos drove the car between double iron gates, expression unrevealing. "Dimitris is the only child in the family, so we must go outside of it for companions for him. We have guests coming from the mainland too, so there's no question of intrusion."

"In that case, I'd very much like to come. "Thank you, *ki*... I mean, Nikos."

His nod was a mite perfunctory. "Think nothing of it."

Sparkling white in the sunlight, the house that came into view was more modern in design than Chelsea would have anticipated—a single storey spreading out in several directions, as if bits had been added almost as afterthoughts. A disappointment in many ways, she had to admit.

Nikos drew up before the arched doorway, but declined to accompany the two of them into the house.

"I'm invited for dinner tonight," he said, "so I'll see you then. *Kali andamosi.*"

The equivalent of "bye for now', Chelsea surmised, not having come across the phrase before. She felt deflated as he headed the car back along the driveway, aware of having made a great deal less than a good start on her campaign—buoying herself up with the thought that she was at least no further away from achieving her aim.

"Come and meet my mother," said Dion. "My father is away on business at present, although he may be back in time for tomorrow's festivities."

If the outside of the house had been a disappointment, the inside was scarcely less so. Lavishly furnished, and heavy on marble and gilt, it left Chelsea with an impression of magazine room settings rather than a home. But then why should these people be expected to conform to her preconceptions simply because they were Greek? she asked herself, following Dion out through the rear of the house to a wide terrace which overlooked an equally spacious swimming pool, with the sea forming a suitable backdrop.

The woman reclining on one of the long, luxuriously padded loungers set beneath a spreading umbrella looked up at her son's approach, her smile taking on a certain resignation as her eyes fell on Chelsea. When she spoke it was in Greek, and too fast for Chelsea to follow, although as Dion didn't look in any way perturbed she could only surmise that the welcome mat hadn't been fully withdrawn.

"This is Chelsea Lovatt from England," he said. "I invited her to stay for a few days before she continues her travels."

"*Khero poli*, Kiria Pandrossos," Chelsea proffered. "I hope I'm not intruding."

"My son's friends are always welcome," returned the other in excellent, if slightly more stilted English than Dion's own, reinforcing what he'd said himself. "Come, take a seat. You are here on holiday?"

"That's right." Chelsea sat down on the nearby chair indicated. "I'm trying to see as many Greek islands as I can before I go home." She gave a smile. "This one wasn't on my itinerary, but I'm grateful for the opportunity to add it to the list."

"Very few foreigners visit Skalos," confirmed her hostess, not unkindly. "Dion, you will order drinks for all of us."

"Of course," he said. "What would you like, Chelsea?"

"A long, cold lemonade would be wonderful," she said.

Chic in a gold-coloured kaftan, her dark hair swept up and back from her face, Kiria Pandrossos relaxed back onto the lounger as her son went back into the house. Dion was her own age, Chelsea already knew, which meant his mother must surely be in her forties, yet she could easily pass for mid-thirties.

"It's easy to see where Dion gets his looks from," she murmured, hardly realising she had spoken out loud until she saw the gratified smile touch the other woman's lips.

"My son and I share many qualities." She paused, viewing the lightly tanned and well-balanced features before her, the cascade of sun-streaked hair. "You are very attractive yourself. But of course you would have to be for Dion to have taken an interest. He is much drawn to blonde hair."

A warning that she wasn't the first and wouldn't be the last, Chelsea sensed. Unnecessary, as it happened, because she had no designs on the man in question. But his mother wasn't to know that.

"I did consider shaving it all off just to see if I still made the same impact," she said, tongue in cheek.

Kiria Pandrossos looked startled for a moment, then relaxed again as she saw the twinkle in the blue eyes opposite. "That would be a drastic experiment indeed. Few men are drawn to bald-headed women, whatever their other looks. Dion would certainly not be one of them."

"I already guessed that," Chelsea assured her, and added impulsively, "He and I are just good friends, and happy to be that way. When I leave, there'll be no heartache on either part."

"Speak for yourself," quoth the subject under discussion, coming out in time to catch the last. "My heart is already broken!"

Chelsea laughed. "It will soon mend."

"English women have no romance in their souls!" he complained, slinging himself down on a lounger. "I'll lie here and pine for what might have been between us!"

Kiria Pandrossos looked as if she found the repartee a little confusing. Obviously unaccustomed to the kind of relationship she and Dion had forged, Chelsea reflected. Kisses were the only form of intimacy they had exchanged—and those themselves light-hearted. They were neither of them looking for any kind of commitment.

The drinks arrived, borne by a youth wearing the seemingly mandatory dark trousers and white shirt of the serving classes in this country. Dion could well have carried them out himself, Chelsea thought, but doubted if the idea would have even occurred to him. Born into money the way he had been, he took service for granted.

"I was not informed that you had called for a car to bring you from the beach, or I would have been expecting you," said Kiria Pandrossos when they each had their glass.

"I didn't call," her son confirmed. "Nikos brought us. He said he would be joining us for dinner tonight."

"Ah, good! He was uncertain of his movements today. Hestia must be told that there will be two more at table."

"Already done." Dion paused to take a drink from his glass. "Florina will be happy to see our cousin."

"As shall we all." His mother sounded faintly reproving. "You must not tease your sister, Dion. Her emotions are too fragile."

"It's Nikos who does the teasing," he retorted. "He knows how she feels for him, but he still holds back!"

"He will speak soon, I am certain. Dimitris needs a mother to care for him when his father is away from home. He must know this."

So Nikos Pandrossos was to marry his cousin, Chelsea reflected, concentrating on her drink. At least, that appeared to be the hope. It would be a good move for the family; there was no doubt. It was Florina she felt sorry for—as she would feel sorry for any woman married to a man like Nikos Pandrossos. An autocrat if ever she saw one!

CHAPTER TWO

LOOKING inland, the bedroom to which she was eventually shown was as sumptuously furnished and decorated as the rest of the house; the wide bed draped in pale lemon silk to match the beautifully hung drapes, the floor carpeted in thickly piled Prussian blue. There was an *en suite* bathroom, complete with a sunken bath convertible to a Jacuzzi at the flick of a switch.

"I could hardly be anything else," Chelsea confirmed when Dion expressed a hope that she would be comfortable. "This is sheer luxury!"

"My mother admires the Italian style of living," he acknowledged. "You'll find Nikos's house very different."

"A traditionalist, is he?" she hazarded.

"If you mean that he prefers the old ways to the new, then, yes."

Chelsea kept her tone light. "With women very much secondary citizens, I take it?"

"Of course. Women are born to serve the male!" Grinning, Dion dodged the pillow she snatched up and slung at him. "*Some* women, at least."

"Does Florina see her role in life that way?" Chelsea felt moved to ask.

"My sister," he said, "will do whatever is necessary to achieve what she desires the most in life."

"To marry Nikos?"

"Yes."

Chelsea sat down on the bed-edge to unzip her bag

and start taking things out, voice casual. "What happened to his wife?"

"The boat in which she and my aunt were returning from a visit to the mainland developed engine trouble and was driven onto rocks in a squall and sank. The crew escaped, but they were trapped below."

"It must have been dreadful for him, losing them both together," said Chelsea, in swift, surging empathy. "How on earth did he cope?"

"The way he copes with everything. No one ever knows Nikos's true feelings." Dion came away from the windowsill, where he had been leaning. "I'll leave you to finish unpacking."

"There's little enough of it to do," she said. "I hope you don't go in for dressing up in the evening, because I'm going to be seriously letting the side down. I set out to travel light."

Dion laughed and shook his head. "We are very informal. Not," he added, "that you could look anything but beautiful whatever you wear. With eyes such as yours, you have no need of jewels!"

"Corn!" Chelsea was laughing too. "Pure, unadulterated corn!"

"It works with others," he returned, unabashed.

She didn't doubt it. Given the opportunity, most would be only too ready to respond to any line he cared to use, however corny. It was a source of some wonder to her still that he left her so relatively unstirred in the physical sense.

His cousin was a different matter, she had to admit. He radiated a sexual attraction impossible to ignore. Not that it made any difference to her prime objective.

So far she had no formulated plan of campaign. The ideal would be to find some way of putting him in her

debt, although she couldn't begin to think how that
might be done. All she could do was play it by ear
and hope for a break of some kind. Being non-
confrontational would be a good start.

Dion was watching her curiously. "You looked just
then as if you had some problem," he remarked. "Is it
one I can help you with?"

"I was just wondering whether to go for a swim before I finish unpacking," she improvised, holding up the
bikini she had just taken out. "If it's all right to use the
pool, that is?"

"Why else would it be there?" he returned. "I'll go
and put on bathing trunks and we'll swim together. You
can find your way back out to the pool?"

"I'm sure of it." Even if it had been a spur-of-the-
moment suggestion, the thought of a dip was tempting.
It was still only just gone six-thirty, and dinner was
hardly likely to be served before nine. Plenty of time to
tidy herself up in. "I'll see you out there," she said.

The blue bikini looked just a little too brief for present
circumstances. She put on a black one-piece suit instead,
missing the fact that the smoothly clinging Lycra out-
lined her shape far more provocatively. An over-sized
white shirt did double duty as a covering wrap; it would
hardly do to parade through the house semi-naked. Her
hair she tied back into her nape with a rubber band.
There would still be plenty of time to wash it before
dinner.

Kiria Pandrossos was gone from the terrace when she
reached it, her place taken by a younger version who
eyed the newcomer with a total lack of welcome.

"You must be Florina," said Chelsea, extending a
smile herself. "I'm Chelsea Lovatt, a friend of Dion's."

"Why are you here?" The question was abrupt.

Chelsea kept the smile going. "Your brother invited me. He'll be out in a moment. We're going to have a swim."

The striking face failed to relax. "Dion treats our home as a hotel! He has no right to bring people here without first asking permission."

"Your mother didn't seem to mind," Chelsea felt bound to respond, and saw the other's expression sour even further.

"My brother can do no wrong in her eyes, but that does not make what he does right."

Sibling jealousy, Chelsea concluded, feeling some sympathy. Sons were all-important in this country. Florina was a year or so older than her brother—of an age when she might be counted as being well and truly on the shelf marriage-wise. Waiting for her cousin to make a move wouldn't have helped. In all fairness, the man should surely clarify his intentions.

Dion's arrival was a relief. If he registered his sister's lack of enthusiasm for their new guest he refused to acknowledge it.

"I'll race you six lengths of the pool," he challenged Chelsea, having already sampled her prowess in the water. "And this time *I* will win!"

Laughing, she slid out of the white shirt and kicked off her sandals, then followed him to the pool-end to pose with him in the classic position. They entered the water in perfect unison, surfacing within seconds of each other and striking out powerfully.

Chelsea had given up competitive swimming on leaving school, but she had kept up the practice because it was one of the best ways of keeping fit. She had little difficulty keeping pace with Dion over the first lengths, and would have beaten him by a short head over the last had her more charitable instincts not caused her to lose just enough ground for him to touch a couple of feet in front. Pandering to male pride, maybe, but it meant far more to him than it did to her.

"You win," she said in mock resignation, treading water.

Curly black hair sparkling with water droplets, *perifania* restored, Dion could afford to be generous. "Only just. You swim faster than any other female I ever encountered! It took me by surprise the first time."

"I know." Tongue tucked firmly in cheek, Chelsea made a wry grimace. "I suppose I'll just have to settle for second best when it comes right down to it."

She turned to swim across the width of the pool to where a metal stepladder extended down into the water, this time using a more restful breast stroke. The sight of the man now seated with Florina on the terrace brought her to an abrupt halt only halfway up the steps. It was too late to drop back into the water because he was looking right at her, mouth taking on the fast-becoming-familiar slant as she vacillated.

He got to his feet to take a towel from the nearby rack and bring it across. Except that instead of placing the towel where she could reach it and retiring again, he opened it up and held it out invitingly, dark eyes cynical.

"*Are* you coming out?" he asked. "Or did you change your mind after all?"

"Coming out." She suited her actions to her words, hauling herself the rest of the way up the ladder and accepting the towel without looking at him directly. Dressed now in beautifully tailored cream trousers and dark brown silk shirt, he was no less disturbing. "Don't let me splash you," she tagged on, hoping he would back off and give her room to breathe.

"Water will do me no harm," he said. "Why did you allow Dion to win just now?"

Feeling considerably more confident with the towel wrapped securely about her, Chelsea raised a pair of innocently widened blue eyes. "Why would I do that?"

"Because of what you hope to gain, perhaps?"

Her brows creased. "Gain?"

"You're far from ingenuous, so don't try playing the part for me," Nikos returned hardily. "Dion may see no further than your face and body, but I'm not so easily blinded. You have a purpose in giving way to him the way you just did—a purpose in being here with him at all, in fact."

Her heart jerked, then steadied again. There was nothing to suggest that he'd guessed the truth. If she read him correctly, his suspicions lay in quite another direction.

"If you think I'm after joining the family, you can forget it," she said bluntly, abandoning discretion for the moment. "Dion won the race on his own merits. Please don't try spoiling it for him by suggesting anything other."

The strongly carved features took on a disquieting expression. "The only suggestion I might—"

He broke off as his cousin hauled himself out of the water at Chelsea's back, obviously not prepared to continue the discussion—if it could rightly be called that—in front of the younger man.

"We didn't expect you until later," said Dion, sounding somewhat less than welcoming to Chelsea's ears.

"I have matters to discuss with your mother," Nikos answered, adding with a certain irony, "If a reason is needed."

His glance came back to Chelsea for a fleeting moment, the message clear to her if to no one else: he hadn't finished with her yet. Then he was moving away, shoulders powerful beneath the brown silk, back tapering down to waist and hip. A hard man in every sense—certainly not one to be trifled with. Chelsea found herself beginning to regret ever having begun this quest.

Hardly a gainful attitude for an ambitious journalist, she rallied. The harder the battle, the more worthwhile the victory. If it all came to nothing in the end, at least she could console herself with the thought that she hadn't given up at the first hurdle. It was up to her to rid Nikos of this notion that she had designs on his cousin for starters.

"What was he saying to you?" asked Dion, jerking her out of her introspection.

"Nothing much," she returned lightly. "I think I'll go and finish unpacking rather than get back in again. I'd like to wash my hair, if there's time."

"We eat at nine," he said. "That gives you almost two hours still."

"Time to spare then."

Sitting alone again, Florina watched her coming with baleful expression. Chelsea gave her a smile in passing, wondering if she was to shoulder the blame for Nikos's disappearance. If he'd wanted to return to the other's side, he would surely have done it.

She saw no sign of him as she made her way to her room, although there were plenty of doors he could be behind. With her own door safely closed, she stood for a moment viewing her image in the long dressing mirror across the room, trying to see herself the way Nikos obviously saw her—coming to the conclusion that he had met so many predatory women in his time he probably took it for granted that they were all at the same game.

One thing he could rely on, she had no designs in that direction where *he* was concerned. She'd as soon stick her head in a tiger's maw!

Showered, hair washed and dried, she fingered through her travelling wardrobe. Consisting, apart from shorts and swimwear, of two crease-proof shift dresses, three skirts, one silky trouser suit and various tops, the choice was limited. In the end she settled on one of the shifts, in a blue almost the same colour as her eyes, contenting herself with a dab of pale pink lipstick and the merest touch of brown mascara. Her only jewellery was a simple gold chain and matching bracelet, which was all she had brought with her.

Weather permitting, meals were always served outside during the warmer months, Dion had already advised. It was still only eight-twenty when she left the room, and apart from a couple of servants no one else was yet in evidence. Emerging once more onto the terrace, she found a table already set out, with aromatic candles lit to deter any flying livestock. The sun was a great golden orb, touching the mainland mountain ridge.

Standing at the stone balustrade, breathing in the evening-scented air and admiring the view, Chelsea felt at peace with the world. The hustle and bustle of life in the city seemed a million miles away. So far she wasn't missing it at all.

The sense of being watched came over her suddenly, lifting the hair at her nape and sending a tingle down her spine. It was no great surprise to turn her head and find Nikos seated on another section of the terrace off to the side of the villa.

"I didn't see you there!" she exclaimed with false brightness.

"Obviously not," he returned drily. He got to his feet, lithe and powerful as any of the big cats in his movements, causing her heart to beat faster and louder as he came towards her. "You would like a drink?"

Chelsea shook her head, feeling stimulated enough at the moment without alcohol. "Not right now, thanks."

"Then perhaps a walk before we eat?"

She looked at him uncertainly, unable to fathom the change in attitude since their last meeting. The dark eyes were impenetrable.

"Why the sudden friendliness?" she asked, deciding to take the bull by the horns, so to speak. "Only a couple of hours ago you were convinced I had designs on your cousin."

"I was perhaps a little hasty in that assessment," came the unfazed reply. "We'll begin again?"

Beware of Greeks bearing gifts, an inner voice urged—except that a change of opinion hardly came under that heading. It took a big man to admit that he might be wrong. If Nikos could bring himself to make the gesture, then she could surely meet him halfway.

"That would be…nice," she said, disgusted by her failure to come up with something a little more inspired. Words were supposed to be her stock-in-trade, for heaven's sake!

"Would it not?" Nikos agreed. "Shall we take the walk I proposed? The gardens are very beautiful at this time of the year. A suitable setting," he tagged on smoothly, "for a beautiful woman. I can find no fault with Dion's taste."

Coming from any other man, Chelsea would have found the compliment too flowery by half, but she couldn't deny the buzz it gave her to hear it from him. Careful, she warned herself. Falling for the man was strictly off-limits—stir parts of her that others had never reached though he undoubtedly did.

"You're too kind," she murmured, and saw a smile touch the firm lips.

"Kindness isn't a quality I'm often accorded."

Chelsea could imagine. Ruthlessness, yes; it was there in every line of those granite features. She had already had a taste of that side of his personality, and was likely to experience it again if she let on what she was really here for too soon.

Just as likely later too, came the thought, pushed to the back of her mind where it could do the least harm.

"I don't suppose it's a quality you can often afford," she said. "Too many people ready to take advantage."

His gaze narrowed a little. "Which people?"

"In business." Chelsea hadn't meant to get this far this fast, but there was no retreating now. "I know who you are, of course. The name Pandrossos is known the world over. Which is why I can't really blame you for thinking I was out to get a foot in the door via Dion. He's what in my part of the world would be called the catch of the century!"

Amusement glinted suddenly in the dark eyes. "You have a turn of phrase that does little credit to the English language at times. I'd be grateful if you took pains not to pass on such terms to my son tomorrow."

"He speaks English at five?"

"The early years are the best time of all to learn. When I'm home, he and I speak English together regularly. The tutor he's to have at the end of the summer will be bilingual too." Nikos paused, shaking his head as if the subject was not one he had intended discussing. "Are we to take our walk?"

Chelsea caught herself up, storing the snippets of background material away for future use. She was still a long way from the goalpost.

"Why not?" she said.

Stretching away on both sides of the house, the gardens proved extensive, with the Italian influence very much in evidence here too. Horticulturally illiterate, even back home, Chelsea had no idea what any of the myriad shrubs and plants were.

"It really is lovely," she remarked, feeling bound to make some comment, however unimaginative, after strolling in silence along the paved paths for several minutes. "So beautifully laid out."

"Selene likes order in every aspect of her life," confirmed Nikos.

"Mistress of the moon," Chelsea murmured, drawing a speculative glance from the man at her side.

"You know something of our mythology?"

"I enjoy dipping into it," she said truthfully. "If memory serves me right, Selene was usurped by Artemis, who killed her lover, Orion, because she thought he was playing around with Eos."

"A generalised interpretation, but not wholly inaccurate. The gods were no more exempt from the desire for vengeance when deceived than we mortals."

Chelsea pulled a leaf from a nearby aromatic shrub, crushing it between her fingers and bringing it to her nose to sniff. "You're saying you might be moved to act the same way under similar circumstances?"

"To kill, no. There are other forms of retribution."

The matter-of-fact statement sent a sudden shiver

down her back. Of a different kind, maybe, but what she was doing could still be classed as deception.

Darkness had fallen, the fireflies flickering in the trees like so many fairylights. Cicadas filled the air with their incessant song.

"Shouldn't we be getting back?" she asked. "It must be almost nine."

"There are still several minutes." Nikos paused at a stone seat set beneath an archway. "We'll sit here for a moment or two and watch the stars emerge."

Other than walking on without him, Chelsea had little choice but to take the seat indicated, feeling the brush of his arm against hers as he sat down beside her. He was too close—too assertively masculine for comfort. Her stomach muscles ached with tension.

"Your hair is luminous in the moonlight," he said softly. "A river of silver!"

"Very poetic," she commented, doing her best to keep her voice steady.

Nikos gave a low laugh. "I appear to be making you nervous."

"You're confusing me," she admitted. "When I arrived on the island you looked at me as if I were some kind of cheap pick-up, then you accused me of making up to Dion with an eye to future prospects, and now..."

"Now?" he prompted as she let the words trail away.

"You tell me," she challenged.

The smile was slow. "Attack is often the best means of defence."

"Against what?"

He made no verbal answer, sliding an arm about her waist to turn her to him, his other hand coming up to circle her nape beneath the heavy fall of hair, eyes glinting as he lowered his head to find her mouth with his.

The kiss left her breathless. He'd made no attempt to do more than just kiss her, yet she'd felt as if every part of her body was under seige.

"Why?" she got out, and saw his lips curve ironically.

"Because I wanted to."

"And you always do exactly as you want to, of course."

"Not always, but some things one cannot deny oneself." His fingers moved caressingly at her nape, bringing her tinglingly alive again. "You have a mouth made for kissing—a body made for loving. Dion could never satisfy you."

Chelsea fought to retain some semblance of control against her treacherous inclinations. If he kissed her again she was going to lose all sense of proportion. "I told you, we don't have that kind of relationship," she said through her teeth. "Just stop this, will you? I'm not available to either of you!"

"I think perhaps you may be, should I care to pursue the matter," Nikos responded, but he let go of her, watching her struggle to contain the involuntary regret with amusement in his eyes. "The flesh is more than willing."

He wasn't far wrong. The desires he had aroused in her were unprecedented. Face burning, she got to her feet, wishing the damned moon would disappear behind a cloud.

"You read a great deal too much into too little," she declared with asperity. "We're going to be late for dinner."

"They will wait."

"I imagine Florina is well used to it where you're concerned," she flashed without pause for reflection, breath catching as the humour was wiped from his face. "I had no right to say that," she mumbled.

"No, you did not," he agreed on a curt note. He rose himself, looming over her. "What has Dion been telling you?"

There was no way out, Chelsea acknowledged ruefully; she had dropped them both right in it.

"Nothing," she said, making the attempt on Dion's behalf at least. "Just something I sensed, that's all. Call it feminine intuition."

"A finely tuned faculty indeed." The satire withered her where she stood. "And what exactly was it that this intuition of yours suggested?"

"Can't we just leave it at that?" she pleaded. "I'm probably completely wrong, anyway."

There was a moment when she thought he was going to insist, then he inclined his head in mocking acknowledgement. "Doubtless. You'd be wise to keep a rein on your imagination."

He turned to start along the path, leaving her to follow in his wake like some reprimanded schoolgirl. To hell with that! she thought, and caught him up, falling into step at his side.

"My stomach's beginning to think my throat's been cut!" she remarked brightly.

Nikos gave her a glance more exasperated than angry. "The only injury sustained thus far is to the spoken word!"

"Sorry." Chelsea put on a penitent expression. "Old habits die hard. I'll do my very best to speak like the Queen from now on." She affected a cut-glass accent. "How now brown cow, and all that."

His laugh was reluctant, but it was a laugh. "You," he said, "need to learn respect!"

What she did need, came the thought, was to be kissed again the way he had kissed her back there; she could still feel the imprint of his lips on hers. A dangerous yearning, considering the effect just the one kiss had had on her. Nikos Pandrossos was not a man to trifle with—in any sphere.

Considering which, the chances of his agreeing to be interviewed once he realised who and what she really was were becoming ever more remote, she had to concede.

"No ready retort?" he taunted.

"Too chastened," she countered, temporarily shelving the problem. "Wasn't that the intention?"

This time the laugh held a note of genuine humour. "It takes more than words to subdue you."

They had reached the foot of the steps leading down from the terrace, viewed with varying expressions by the group gathered there as they mounted into the light. Chelsea could only be thankful that her lipstick was the non-transferable variety—although Nikos couldn't have known that. If the thought had occurred to him at all, it didn't appear to be causing him any concern.

"Tell Hestia she can begin serving now," Selene Pandrossos directed her daughter, with what Chelsea considered admirable constraint. "We were beginning to think you had spirited our guest away, Nikos."

"I wanted to see the gardens before it went dark," Chelsea rushed in before he could answer. "Kirios Pandrossos was kind enough to take me round. It's entirely my fault that we've held things up."

"It's been dark for the past half an hour," put in Dion, making no attempt to disguise his scepticism.

"The gardens are very large," countered his cousin imperturbably.

"And very beautiful," Chelsea confirmed.

Looking beautiful herself in virginal white, Florina eyed her with open hostility. Chelsea could hardly blame her for feeling that way. Had she been kept dangling on a string for years, only to see the object of her desire usurped by another woman, and a foreigner at that, she would have felt the same. It would be a waste of time telling her that she had no interest in her cousin.

It was hardly true anyway—in any sense.

CHAPTER THREE

NEVER a hasty event, and taking the late start into consideration, the meal went on until well gone midnight. All conversation was conducted in English, in deference to the guest, which made Chelsea feel even more of an outsider. Seated between Kiria Pandrossos and Dion at the big round table, with Nikos directly opposite, she was constantly aware of the dark eyes on her. Florina was by no means blind to the fact either, she reckoned.

Fending off questions about her background wasn't easy. More than once she found herself on the brink of admitting the truth and accepting the consequences. That she didn't was largely because of Dion, who would be devastated to discover how he'd been used. In all fairness, he had to be put in the picture first—*and* exonerated from any blame if and when the occasion arose.

It was almost twelve-thirty when Nikos departed. Kiria Pandrossos took her leave too, followed almost immediately by Florina, with a cursory response to Chelsea's *"kalinichta'*.

"She's distressed over Nikos," explained Dion unnecessarily. "Because he spent so much time alone with you in the gardens." He eyed her speculatively. "You looked disquieted when you returned."

Not so much shaken as stirred, thought Chelsea with assumed flippancy.

"Your cousin's an intimidating man," she said. "Difficult to relax with."

"Yet you asked him to accompany you?"

36

"A spur-of-the-moment idea because I couldn't think of anything else to say," she improvised, not about to acknowledge that the suggestion had come from him. "I didn't expect to find him out here on his own."

"He wouldn't have been alone if Florina had known."

"I'm sure." Chelsea twirled the stem of her wine glass between finger and thumb for a moment before lifting it to drain the last of the contents, placing it back on the table to add tentatively, "Do you think he will eventually make the move?"

"To marry her?" Dion lifted his shoulders. "With Nikos, who can tell?"

"If he really does know how she feels about him, it's hardly right of him to let her go on hoping if he has no intention."

The shrug came again. "You heard me say that to him in the car earlier."

"I heard you say that she hoped to be married in the not too distant future," Chelsea conceded. "I didn't realise at the time that it was aimed at him."

"Nikos would have known it."

"Then hints obviously aren't enough. Someone should try telling him straight."

Dion gave her a bland smile. "If you're so concerned for my sister's welfare, perhaps you should do it yourself."

Already tried, already failed, she could have told him. She laughed and shook her head. "I'll pass on that one."

"I thought you might." He drained his own glass, indicating the still half full bottle of wine. "You'd like some more?"

Chelsea shook her head. "Not for me, thanks. In fact, I think I'll be off to bed, if you don't mind?"

"I'm desolated," he claimed, looking slightly put out. "No other girl ever treated me the way you do. Do I not make your heart beat even a little bit faster?"

"Of course you do," she soothed, recognising wounded male vanity when she heard it. "I'd have to be blind not to find you outstandingly attractive."

"But you've no desire to share your bed with me?"

"I don't share a bed with any man," she said firmly. "I thought we had all that clear."

The grin was reassuring. "We do, but I'm only flesh and blood. It's man's nature to desire a beautiful woman. Nikos was stirred by you himself; *that* much I could read of his thoughts. Never has he looked at Florina the way he looked at you tonight. He demanded to know earlier if the two of us were lovers already."

Chelsea tried to keep an even tone. "And what did you tell him?"

"That we were just friends. Not that he believed it. 'Between a man and a woman,' he said, 'there is no such thing as just friends.'" Dion paused, eyeing her with the same speculation he had employed before. "Do you find him attractive?"

What Nikos made her feel went far beyond mere attraction, she acknowledged, remembering those tumultuous moments in his arms.

"As I already said, I find him thoroughly intimidating," she claimed, not without truth. "He isn't nearly as good-looking as you."

"He's older, and many women prefer older men. Especially when they're wealthy too."

"I don't care about money," Chelsea returned, truthfully again. "I've enough of my own to get by on."

She paused, tempted once more to let Dion in on her secret. There was a possibility that he might feel honour-bound to give her away, but she doubted it. There was little love lost between him and Nikos.

"There's something I have to tell you," she said, before she could change her mind. "A confession, I suppose you'd have to call it."

The speculation increased. "So tell me?"

"I'm a journalist." It came out in a rush. "I should have been honest with you right away, I know, but when you asked me to come here with you it was too good an opportunity to put at risk. No one's ever managed to interview your cousin. I'm hoping to be the first."

Viewing the handsome, and at the moment inscrutable face, she knew a gathering despondency. "I shan't blame you if you feel like telling me to take off," she added. "No one likes being used."

"No, they don't." The agreement was severe, the scowl even more so. "You should be ashamed!"

"I know," she said. "I took a mean advantage."

Dion studied her for a moment, the mock anger replaced by a certain calculation. "No more than I intended taking of you," he said at length. "And still intend, if you prove willing." He shook his head at the look on her face. "Not that. I asked you here for quite another purpose."

Intrigued enough to forget her own position for the moment, Chelsea eyed him questioningly. "What purpose?"

"There's this girl," he said. "A daughter of one of the families allowed to share Skalos. I want her to think that you and I are an item—isn't that the way you say it?"

"It's the way some people say it." She paused. "What is it you're after, exactly?"

"I intend to show her she's far from my only interest," he stated with a flash of fire in his eyes.

Pride rearing its head again? Chelsea reflected.

"Why would you need me for that?" she asked. "You must have a whole list of girls you could call on."

"Those who would like to be with me, yes."

But none likely to agree to being used as a mere instrument, Chelsea surmised. At least it explained why Dion had been so ready to accept the limitations she had imposed on their own relationship.

"Having already told Nikos there's nothing between us, isn't it going to make you appear more than a bit of a liar if we start putting on an act for this girl's benefit?" she said cautiously, thinking it wasn't going to do her credibility much good either.

"We don't have to put on an act," he assured her. "It will be enough for Elini to see us together."

Enough for what? Chelsea wondered. "I suppose I owe you something for not being honest with you from the start," she said with some reluctance.

"If you do this for me, I'll do everything I can to help you get what *you* want," Dion promised. An innate decency prompted him to add, "Although I should warn you that there's very little possibility of success. Nikos despises those who put themselves on public display. Nor would I advise attempting to publish anything without permission."

"I wouldn't do that anyway." Chelsea could make that promise in all honesty. "I knew the odds were against me when I took this on, but it was worth a try. Still is," she added, stiffening her resolve. "There has to be a first time for everything."

Dion came to his feet along with her, a certain regret

in his eyes as he scanned her face. "Must you really sleep alone tonight?"

"Really," she said. She kissed him lightly on the cheek. "*Kalinichta,* friend."

He made no effort to stop her as she turned to go indoors, but she could sense frustration in him. Nikos was probably right, she thought drily: there was no such thing as a purely platonic relationship between a man and a woman—certainly not where the man was concerned, at any rate.

In bed, but unable to sleep, she found her thoughts dwelling on Nikos again, seeing him in her mind's eye, features sculpted from solid rock, body taut with muscle, remembering the feel of his lips on hers, the power to crush in his hands. She hadn't known what it was to desire a man until now, because she had never before met a man who aroused her to such an extent. For the first time she could understand that love didn't *have* to be a part of the equation.

Taking account both of what he had said to her in the gardens and the expression in his eyes every time she had met his gaze during the rest of the evening, there was every reason to believe that he found her equally desirable. If she couldn't find fulfilment in one direction, she might at least...

She broke off her thoughts at that point, shocked that she could even contemplate such a move. There was such a thing as moral fibre.

Morning brought no change in Florina's attitude. Chelsea gave up trying after receiving monosyllabic replies to all her overtures.

The skies were clear of any vestige of cloud, the rising heat tempered by a gentle breeze blowing in from the sea. Despite enjoying a lazy morning alongside Dion on the terrace, she knew it wouldn't take long to become bored with the easy life. She needed to be up and do-ing—to have something to keep both body *and* mind active.

The party was due to begin at four. Dion's father still hadn't put in an appearance when they left the house on the hour. Dion was driving, with his mother occupying the front passenger seat, leaving Chelsea to share the rear with his sister. The latter spoke not a single word during the journey, gazing steadfastly out of the window, her face set in lines that warned off any attempt to start a conversation.

Compared with the *haute couture* outfits both the Pandrossos women were wearing, the silky black trou-sers and sleeveless top Chelsea had on were definitely second-rate, but they were the only things she had with her that were even remotely suitable to the occasion. Beggars couldn't be choosers, she told herself stoutly. Who was going to be taking any notice, anyway? This was Dimitris's day.

Their destination lay barely a couple of miles away around the other side of the headland. Reached through olive groves, the house drew a breath of delight. Creeper-covered white walls nestled beneath a faded red roof, each tall and graceful window flanked by dark blue shutters. Big enough to house several families, Chelsea judged, but still looking like a home rather than a show-place.

They were not the first arrivals. Several cars were al-ready parked around the gravelled area fronting the house. Dion slid an arm around Chelsea's waist as they entered a spacious hall which appeared to go all the way through to the rear of the building, where tall double doors were folded back to reveal a magnificent, uninterrupted view of the sea.

"I thought we didn't have to pretend anything," she said out of the corner of her mouth.

"No more we do," he confirmed, but he made no attempt to remove the arm, steering her in the direction of the rear exit with his mother and sister following on behind.

The doorway gave on to an iron-railed terrace, from which a flight of stone steps led down to a wide, paved courtyard brilliant with spilling plant life. There were several umbrella-shaded tables, but the majority of people gathered down there were standing around in small groups. The shouts and screams associated with young people enjoying themselves could clearly be heard, although they were nowhere to be seen.

"They'll be down on the lower level," Dion supplied, anticipating the question. He indicated the stone archway at the far end of the courtyard. "Through there. The gardens are built on several levels down to the shore. Nikos will have organised entertainment on one of the lawns so that they don't injure themselves."

He scrutinised the groups below, his grasp tensing a little as he found what he sought. "There's Elini. The one in red."

Chelsea followed his gaze, coming to rest on a curvaceous young figure in a bright red dress that showed off the cloud of black hair to its best advantage. No more than eighteen, she judged, studying the captivating face; something of a flirt too, if the way she was smiling up at the young man next to her was anything to go by.

Kiria Pandrossos and Florina had already descended to greet friends and neighbours. Chelsea allowed herself to be drawn down the steps, fixing a smile on her face as Dion proceeded to introduce her to people. The response appeared genial enough on the surface, though she sensed a certain reticence in some. It was only to be expected, she supposed, that not everyone would welcome a foreigner in their midst on a purely Greek occasion.

The group Elini was with Dion left till the last. Chelsea attempted to weigh up the girl's reaction when they were introduced, but saw little sign that her presence was arousing any jealousy—assuming that was what Dion was after.

She stiffened involuntarily as someone came up behind her, knowing who it was even before he spoke.

"Come and meet my son," said Nikos, making it sound as much like a command as an invitation. "He'll be delighted to practise his English on you." His smile encompassed the rest of the group, Dion included. "*Signomi, parakalo.*"

They were halfway across the patio before Chelsea drew breath. Nikos wasn't touching her in any way—wasn't even all that close—yet she could feel the sun-stoked heat of his body radiating through the white slacks and shirt he was wearing. Only the women had bothered to dress up, she had already noted, the men opting for comfort rather than style.

"It's a lovely day for it," she remarked, driven once more to say something—*anything*.

"For what?" Nikos queried without particular inflexion.

"A child's birthday party. So much better if it can be held outdoors, where they can let off steam without creating havoc. I mean, no matter how good they are normally, kids tend to get over-excited on occasions like this. I can remember my mother going spare over the mess my guests used to create!'' She was babbling and she knew it, but she couldn't seem to stop. ''Of course, you don't have to cater for weather variations to quite the same extent we do back home. People even take out insurance against having an event rained off.''

''With very short odds, I imagine,'' Nikos commented drily. He glanced her way, eyebrow lifting. ''Do you have anything more to say on the subject?''

Chelsea pulled a rueful face. ''I'm not always so garrulous.''

''But with me you have to talk in an effort to conceal what I make you feel.''

They had reached the archway. Down another flight of steps lay a walled and grassed area where what appeared at first glance to be several dozen children were whooping it up with a whole troupe of clowns. Nikos made no immediate move to descend, studying her face with unconcealed amusement.

''So assured on the surface, so timorous beneath,'' he taunted. ''Would you deny your response to me?''

Several suitably flippant replies raced through Chelsea's mind, all of them discarded. The only way to deal with this situation was to answer in like vein.

''Not for a moment,'' she said. ''I'm sure there's no woman alive whose heart fails to palpitate when you're around.''

''Ah, but not all women stir *me* the way you do.'' His voice had lowered, infinitely seductive in its caressing intonation.

''Tough!'' she shot back at him, determined to keep her end up. ''As I told you last night, I'm not on the market.''

''Last night was last night.'' Eyes glinting in the sunlight, he indicated the steps. ''Shall we go down?''

Conscious that several pairs of eyes were on them, Chelsea took the line of least resistance. At least there would be no more such talk with children in the vicinity. Time to unravel her stomach muscles and get a hold of herself.

A small, wiry figure emerged from the general throng as the two of them reached the bottom of the steps, tearing across to issue a breathless greeting. Dressed in shorts and T-shirt, as were most of the children, black hair cut short to control a riotous curl, he had a positively angelic little face, every feature exquisitely defined.

Not bothering to wait for Nikos to perform formal introductions, Chelsea gave the boy a broad smile. "Hallo, Dimitris, my name is Chelsea." She held out the small package she had been toting around. "Happy birthday!"

Looking a little nonplussed, the boy waited for his father's nod before accepting the present, not forgetting to say, *"Efcharisto."* He showed the usual childish impatience in tearing off the wrappings, viewing the hand-sized LCD pinball game enclosed with puzzled eyes.

Forgetting Nikos for the moment, Chelsea squatted at the boy's side to show him how to use the game, sparking an eager desire to try it for himself. Next moment he was racing off to show the machine to his friends, gathering a little crowd about him, all clamouring for a go.

"Thank you," said Nikos as Chelsea straightened. "You appear to have a very good idea of what appeals to small boys."

Big boys too, she thought with irony. The difference being that she wasn't out to gratify the latter.

"Just a token," she said. "Makes me feel a bit less of a gatecrasher."

Nikos gave her a quizzical look. "You were invited."

"Only because common courtesy made it impossible for you to do anything else."

"True," he agreed. "But it was no great hardship. Your presence would enhance any occasion."

"Such a gentleman!" she muttered, and saw his mouth stretch into a slow smile.

"Not always, *ylikia.*"

What *"ylikia"* meant, Chelsea had no idea. Nor did she care to ask. She turned her attention a little desperately to the group of young women seated together around a table in a far corner. "Are they the children's nannies?"

"Nurses, yes. One of them Dimitris's."

"Do you have to leave him often?" she asked. "On business, I mean."

"No more than I must. A boy needs a father."

"More than he needs a mother?"

The chiselled features were suddenly austere. "Is this another attempt to tell me what I should do?"

"No, of course not." Chelsea bit back the apology hovering on her lips. "I don't suppose he remembers his mother at all."

"He was barely two years old when she died. How could he remember her?"

"Probably as well that he was too young to realise," she ventured. "It must have been dreadful for you."

"It was a long time ago," came the abrupt reply.

His wife's death would obviously be the last thing he wanted to discuss today of all days, Chelsea thought ruefully, regretting ever having brought the subject up. She had been moved by genuine empathy, with no journalistic undertones, but it had still been a tactless thing to do.

"One of these days I'll learn when to keep my mouth shut," she said on wryly humorous note. "About the same time hell freezes over, as certain people might be moved to say."

The strong mouth twitched. "It isn't difficult to stop a woman from talking too much. A gag is very effective. Not," he added on a reassuringly lightened note, "that I'd consider such methods myself. There are other ways."

Chelsea could imagine. She'd experienced one of them last night. Almost as if in direct response to her thoughts, Nikos put out a hand and smoothed a fingertip down her small straight nose to come to rest momentarily on her lips, registering her reaction with a mocking glint.

"See how you tremble to my touch!"

"One thing you're not short of is ego," she muttered, drawing a deep, infinitely attractive laugh.

"It's a poor man who fails to recognise desire in a woman. It happened between us the moment our eyes met yesterday."

"I'd have said instant antagonism myself," Chelsea parried, aware that she was way out of her depth with this man.

He laughed again, obviously enjoying himself. "A little antagonism only adds spice to an affair."

"It might if there was going to be one," she retorted, with what assurance she could infuse into her voice. "Can we stop playing games now?"

A spark leapt in the dark eyes. "I only play games with children. *You* are not a child."

So far as this kind of thing went she was a babe in arms, Chelsea reflected, giving up even trying to keep pace. Looking at him, senses stirred by his sheer masculine presence, she was unable to deny a temptation to let matters take their natural course. It would mean abandoning all hope of attaining her original aim, but, as Dion had said, the chances were remote to start with.

The question was, dare she?

The answer was, not if she had any sense left at all.

"I have an absolutely raging thirst," she heard herself saying. "Could we go and get a drink?"

"But of course." Nikos was smiling, not in any way deceived. "Whatever you wish."

CHAPTER FOUR

ONE of the servants approached as they reached the patio. Catching the word *telephono,* Chelsea was already prepared when Nikos turned to tell her he had to leave her for the present.

"I can get myself a drink," she assured him. "Or Dion can get me one," she added, seeing the latter moving towards them.

The banter vanished now, Nikos gave a brief nod and started for the house, leaving her uncertain whether relief or regret held the upper hand at the moment.

"I gather things aren't going quite the way you planned," she commented to a disgruntled-looking Dion.

"Is that surprising when you spend more time with Nikos than you do with me?" he returned sourly.

"I could hardly tell him I didn't want to meet Dimitris," Chelsea protested.

"That would have taken only a few minutes. You were gone almost half an hour!"

"One doesn't walk away from one's host."

"It will do you no good," he warned. "Nikos may find you an attraction now, but it will be a different matter when he discovers why you're really here."

Chelsea eyed him in silence for a moment, wrestling with the inner conflict. "There isn't going to be any need for him to know," she said at length. "I'm giving up on the idea."

Disgruntlement gave way to surprise. "So soon?"

Her shrug was rueful. "It was a bad idea to start with. He's entitled to his privacy. I'll go back to the original plan and write about touring the islands instead. There's always a market for travel articles."

"But you'll stay here on Skalos a few more days?"

Chelsea hesitated again, knowing what common sense dictated. "I can't see how my staying on is going to do any good. Elini didn't seem too upset to see you with someone else."

More explicit than any words, the expression that crossed Dion's face pulled her up short in sudden realisation. She said softly, "It's more than just pride, isn't it? You're in love with her."

"She makes me crazy," he admitted. "Others are eager enough to be with me!"

"Hasn't she ever shown any interest in you at all?" Chelsea asked sympathetically.

"Not in me alone." He made a fierce gesture. "I share with no other man!"

"Perhaps if you made your feelings clear to her it would be different."

"And have her tell everyone she has Dion Pandrossos begging her favours!"

"I'm sure she wouldn't do that." Chelsea couldn't be sure at all, but it seemed the only way of resolving the impasse. "It could even be what she's waiting for. Taking it that you do have serious intentions towards her," she added with purpose. "You hardly gave that impression last night when you wanted to take me to bed."

"That was just sex," he said dismissively. "It meant nothing."

Chelsea was aware of it, though the casual acknowledgment still knocked her back. "If you feel the way you say you do about her, you shouldn't even be thinking of making love with anyone else,'' she returned, curbing the urge to sock him on his handsome jaw. ''Man's nature or not!''

Like water off a duck's back, she thought resignedly, seeing no discernible appreciation in the dark eyes. He heard what she was saying, but it made little difference to his attitude.

Let's go get a drink,'' she said, giving up. ''I could grow cacti on my tongue!''

Dion grinned, problems momentarily forgotten. ''I've never known anyone who says things the way you do! Come and see what you would like.''

What she'd like more than anything was for Nikos to see her as something other than a mere sex object himself, Chelsea acknowledged as they moved in the direction of the bar set up under the house wall. Some women were capable of viewing sex the same way most men viewed it—an experience to be enjoyed as and when desired without commitment of any kind—but she doubted if she could ever be one of them. There had to be something more than lust.

For a brief moment back there, when Nikos had looked down at his son, she had caught a glimpse of the inner man. But even if she stayed a few more days on the island it was unlikely that she'd be given the opportunity to plumb those hidden depths. For all she knew, he wouldn't be here after today anyway.

Whether it was because Nikos had shown a personal interest in her, or simply that she'd misread attitudes earlier, she couldn't be sure, but there was no sign of standoffishness now. Everyone spoke English to a greater or lesser degree, and made light of her lack of aptitude in their own language.

Nikos returned to the patio as the children were

brought up to eat their fill from the loaded buffet tables. He looked distracted, Chelsea thought, watching him as he moved among the gathering. Business problems, perhaps? No company, however successful, was immune from trouble.

"Is it Dion or Nikos who has your interest?" asked a voice at her elbow, and she turned with a start to see Elini regarding her inscrutably.

Dion was off refilling glasses, and for the moment the two of them had the table to themselves. Chelsea hesitated before replying, uncertain of her ground.

"Which would you prefer?" she hedged at length.

"I would like it best if you were not here at all," came the candid response.

Tell the truth and shame the devil! Chelsea reflected in wry amusement. "Why?" she asked, plumping for the same direct approach.

"You do not belong on Skalos." The lovely young face was still quite calm, but there was a spark in the girl's eyes. "You should stay with your own kind."

"Nationality or sex?" Chelsea queried mildly, and saw the spark flare into flame.

"English girls have no shame! They allow a man liberties no Greek girl would think of!"

Personal observation, or simply hearsay? Chelsea wondered. "Some might," she conceded, refraining from pointing out that vacational promiscuity was by no means confined to the English. "We're not all tarred with the same brush."

Elini eyed her sceptically. "You are saying you have never made love with Dion?"

"That's right." It was taking a liberty Dion almost certainly wouldn't approve of, but there was more to this attack than simple xenophobia. "I'm here because he wanted to make a certain person jealous, that's all. He was very cut up when it didn't seem to be working."

Dark eyes took on a new expression. "Which person?"

Chelsea smiled, hoping she was reading this right. "You must know how he feels about you."

"Dion likes many girls," came the slow reply.

"But not in the same way."

"He told you this?"

Chelsea took new heart from the suddenly lighter note in the younger girl's voice. "To put it in his own words—you make him crazy."

Elini gave a laugh, her whole demeanour altering. "Then the magazines are right!"

"If they told you to play hard to get, it seems to have worked," Chelsea agreed. For how long was another question, came the mental rider.

"Do you love him?" she asked, thinking it was bit late to turn diffident now.

Animosity completely vanished, Elini sparkled back at her. "Who could not?"

"You'd like to marry him?"

"Of course." What else? the tone suggested.

The Pandrossos name would be a draw in itself, Chelsea suspected—where the girl's parents were concerned, at any rate. On the face of it, Dion could do a lot worse. The question was whether Elini might do better to find herself a husband with a proper sense of responsibility. Dion had never worked for his living; he had already told her that. Whatever he needed was supplied for him by his mother, who was apparently wealthy in her own right. Whether the latter would also be willing to support a wife was another matter.

"You look doubtful," Elini observed, sounding just a

shade truculent again. "You think there is little hope of it?"

"Not at all," Chelsea assured her without undue emphasis. "I think any man would count himself fortunate to have you for a wife. All the same," she added, "I'd keep him guessing a little longer if I were you."

"I will try." Smiling once more, Elini got to her feet. "I had better go before he comes back and finds me here with you. I am grateful to you, Chelsea."

Chelsea smiled back constrainedly, wishing now that she had left well alone. If the union was meant to be it would have come about without her interference. How could she even be sure that Dion's feelings for the girl were genuine and lasting?

It was something of a relief that he made no mention of having seen the two of them together on his return. From now on, she vowed, she would keep her nose out of other people's affairs.

Those who had brought young children along began drifting away around seven, most with a journey back to the mainland to face. The ones left looked set for the evening.

"While ever there are people here," Dion confirmed when Chelsea asked how long things were likely to go on for. His eyes were on Elini, who was laughing over something the same young man she had been with earlier was saying to her, his scowl indicative of his feelings.

"Why don't you go and oust him?" Chelsea suggested, forgetting her pledge. "You're not going to get anywhere by standing here glowering at the pair of them."

"I compete with no man!" he declared, turning the scowl on her. "I already told you that."

Just *when* would she learn to stop meddling? Chelsea

asked herself ruefully. "Sorry," she said. "Forget I spoke." She adopted a lighter note. "Anyway, I need to find a bathroom."

Nikos had made no further attempt to seek her company since being called away, and she saw nothing of him as she made her way indoors. It was pretty obvious that he'd lost interest in her as a game worth pursuing any further, for which she couldn't blame him. What did she have that he couldn't get from other women—and with far less effort?

She would cut her losses and head out again tomorrow, she decided. Put the whole episode behind her. It had been a pipe dream to start with.

Furnished throughout in the dark carved wood that stood so well against plain white walls, the house met almost every traditional criterion. Chelsea loved the stark simplicity of it, so different from the other Pandrossos home.

Washing her hands in a well-equipped bathroom she found on the upper floor, she tried to imagine Florina living here, failing because the image just didn't fit. Considering the lack of attention Nikos had paid to his cousin this afternoon, the chances of her doing so seemed pretty remote anyway. It was possible that Florina and her mother had been deceiving themselves all along.

All the same, Dimitris should have a mother. A nurse was no substitute. The child had been brought indoors some time ago, and would probably be fast asleep by now, dreaming of the day just spent. Chelsea would have liked to say goodbye, but it wasn't to be. There was nothing to be gained from it anyway.

The door opposite had been closed when she went into the bathroom. It was ajar when she emerged, revealing a bed on a side wall of the room within. The small, dark-haired boy sitting up in it had his attention concentrated on something he held in his hands.

Her own present to him, Chelsea realised in some gratification, hearing the beeps. A simple thing, yet obviously of absorbing interest if he'd sneaked it into bed with him.

He appeared to be alone at present. On impulse, she moved across and tapped lightly on the door, smiling as the dark head jerked up.

"Hallo, Dimitris," she said. "Not sleepy yet?"

Recognition was instant, the answering smile wide. "It's still my birthday," he said. "When I go to sleep it will be over. I don't want it to be over."

Bilingual at five years of age! Chelsea marvelled, admiring the child's command and clear enunciation. If his prowess in that direction was anything to go by, he had to be way above average intelligence. But then, with Nikos Pandrossos for a father it was unlikely that he'd be anything other.

"Doesn't your nurse stay with you until you're asleep?" she asked, making no move to go further into the room.

"Ledra is visiting with Stavros." Dimitris said it matter-of-factly.

"Who is Stavros?" Chelsea felt bound to enquire.

"He works in the gardens. He has a little house there. I like your present very much," Dimitris added, obviously seeing little of interest in the foregoing. "Would you like to play with it too?"

Chelsea hesitated only a moment before pushing the door wider and going on in. There was surely no harm in keeping the boy company for a while—especially as

his nurse appeared to have deserted him for more allur-
ing interests.

"I'm not much good at this sort of thing," she confessed, perching on the edge of the bed to take the game
from him. "I tried it out when I bought it, but I couldn't
get a very high score."

"I can," claimed Dimitris, and clambered free of the
bedclothes in order to perch on his knees, where he
could watch over her shoulder. "You're very slow," he
observed judiciously as she pressed the various keys.

"Poor co-ordination." Chelsea groaned as the num-
bers came up on screen. "I've done worse than ever!"

Her small companion patted her shoulder comfort-
ingly. "You may try again, if you wish."

Chelsea shook her head and handed the little machine
back. "Show me what you can do."

He did, hands dancing like lightning over the keys,
the deeper bleeps registering scores coming fast and fu-
rious. They were both of them too engrossed to be aware
of the man who paused in the open doorway to view
dark and light heads pressed so close together.

"You're simply too good for this!" exclaimed
Chelsea when the final score showed maximum points.
"Have you ever used a computer?"

"Five is too young for computers," said Nikos, bringing both heads up and round in unison.

Dimitris said something in Greek, too fast for Chelsea
to grasp, bringing a fleeting amusement to his father's
face. "It appears," he declared, "that my opinion isn't
shared."

"Some children show an early aptitude," Chelsea responded. "I hope you don't mind my being here," she
added diffidently. "There was someone in the down-

stairs bathroom, so I came up to look for another. The door was open, and Dimitris was awake.''

"I didn't imagine you would have woken him yourself," came the dry rejoinder. "Where is Ledra?"

Chelsea held her breath as she waited for Dimitris to answer that one, but he made no attempt, attention once more on the game. "I haven't seen her," she was bound to admit. "But I've only been here a few minutes myself."

Dimitris spoke again in Greek, the inflexion hopeful, but this time his father shook his head.

"Tomorrow," he said. "This is the time for sleep."

Whatever the request had been, the child accepted the refusal with good grace. Probably, Chelsea thought, because he knew he would get nowhere by protesting. She made an automatic move to tuck him in again as he slid back beneath the bedclothes, only just stopping herself from dropping a swift kiss on the thicket of black curls. Her cheeks burned as she straightened to meet Nikos's speculative gaze.

"You appear to be well accustomed to putting a child to bed," he observed.

"I take care of my sister's two sometimes," she acknowledged. "It was purely instinctive."

"As it should be in a woman," he said softly. "I think you perhaps play the modernist more for effect than from belief."

Chelsea summoned a flippant note. "Meaning I'm really just a sweet old-fashioned girl underneath?"

His lips quirked. "I wouldn't go quite that far."

Looking from one to the other with bright-eyed interest, Dimitris appeared to be sensing the undercurrents. Chelsea stirred herself to get up, judging it was time to take her leave.

"Goodnight, Dimitris," she said, directing a smile at the child. "Sleep tight!"

"I wish *you* were my nurse, not Ledra," was the unanticipated response.

Hardly knowing what to reply to that, Chelsea settled for a laugh, ruffling the dark head with a pang of regret that this was likely to be the last time she saw him. She had told the truth yesterday when she'd said she didn't like all children. There were even times when her sister's somewhat over-indulged pair were a little too much. Dimitris was something else. Like his father, he exerted a nigh on irresistible pull.

Nikos took the pinball game from him and placed it out of reach before following Chelsea from the room and closing the door.

"You gained my son's trust very quickly," he observed.

"For a foreigner, you mean?" she answered lightly, and saw his lips slant.

"Children place little importance on such things. They see the person inside."

Not the whole of her, thank heaven, came the wry thought. Any journalistic aspirations regarding the Pandrossos family had flown, but who would believe it if the truth came out? Dion could, and probably would expose her if he discovered that she had given *him* away. Hopefully, Elini could be relied on to keep her own counsel on that score—at least until after Chelsea had left the island.

"I'd better get back down in case Kiria Pandrossos is ready to go," she said. "We all came in the one car."

"Because you came in the one car, it isn't necessary to return in the one car," Nikos responded levelly. "I want you to stay."

Looking into the dark eyes, Chelsea felt her heart lurch, her pulses quicken. "You have other guests."

"They don't hold the same interest for me." He reached for her, drawing her closer to cup her face between his hands, thumbs gently smoothing her lips. "I want you, *ylikia*. As you want me too. Are we to deny ourselves the pleasure?"

"What are you suggesting?" she demanded huskily, struggling to contain the urge to throw caution to the four winds and go for what her every sense told her would be the experience of a lifetime. "That we find a bed right now?"

The laugh came low. "It would satisfy neither of us to spend a mere hour together. I wish to spend the whole of the night with you."

"That's hardly possible." There was a very large part of her that only wished it was.

"Nothing is impossible," he returned, with the arrogance of one who had never known failure in any sphere of life. "If we wish it, we make it happen."

Trying to make out that she had no desires in that direction herself would be a waste of time, Chelsea accepted. He knew exactly how he made her feel: the same way he would have made many other women feel in his time. If he'd still had a wife there would have been no question, of course—on her side at any rate. As it was...

Her thought processes blurred as he bent his head to find her lips with his, her senses concentrated on that vibrant point of contact. He drew her closer, hands creating havoc as they moved over her slender curves, burning like fire through the silky film of her clothing.

Because of the heat, she was wearing little beneath the garment. She felt his reaction when he found her breasts unconfined by any brassière, heard him say something she couldn't catch under his breath. The hand shifted downwards to seek the bottom edge of the loose tunic top, sliding up again over tremoring bare flesh to encircle the firm swell. Chelsea had never known a sensation as exquisite as the touch of those long, tensile fingers. Her inner thigh muscles contracted, starting a chain reaction right through her body.

Her hand lifted of its own volition to grasp his wrist and still the movement. "No more!" she managed to gasp out. "Please, Nikos. Enough!"

"For now," he said softly, removing the hand. "This is not the place, I agree. But I *will* have you, *ylikia*."

"Only if I agree to be had!"

Nikos smiled as she drew away from him, making no attempt to stop her. "You will agree because you want to agree. Because your body won't allow you to say no to me."

"Mind can govern matter!" she shot back, serving only to widen the smile.

"We shall see."

This had to stop, Chelsea told herself resolutely, and it had to stop right here! "No, we won't," she said. "I'm leaving Skalos tomorrow."

"To leave so soon after arrival would be regarded as a slur on my aunt's hospitality. Would you have her insulted?"

"If anything, I think she'd be glad to see the back of me. I'm sure Florina would."

The olive-skinned features tautened, humour vaporising. "I asked last night; now I ask again. What is this concern of yours for Florina?"

For "ask', in this instance read "demand', Chelsea reckoned, seeing the glint in his eyes. So, all right, let him have it.

"You must know how she feels about you," she said. "Don't you think you've kept her dangling long enough?"

"I'm aware of what both she and her mother have had in mind for the past three years," he acknowledged curtly. "But that places me under no obligation to comply. If I decide to take another wife, I will do the choosing myself this time!"

He caught himself up, as if aware of having already said more than intended, adding on a forcible note, "Forget about Florina. She has no relevance."

The intimation that his marriage had been arranged had driven everything else from mind for the moment. Of all people, Chelsea would have thought this man the last to accede to that particular custom. It didn't necessarily mean that he hadn't loved Dimitris's mother, but the emotion wasn't mandatory to such an arrangement.

Whichever, it made little difference to her own situation. All he wanted with her was one night. He wasn't going to get it, of course. The obvious difficulties aside, she'd be a fool to allow herself that degree of involvement with a man who could tilt the world on its axis with a mere caress.

"Better still, let's forget the whole thing," she said flatly, shutting out the small dissenting voice. "I'll get Dion to run me back to Skiathos in the morning, and carry on from there."

His shrug was brief, his expression unreadable. "If that's what you want."

It wasn't so much what she wanted as what she didn't dare *not* do, Chelsea reflected wryly as he indicated that they proceed in the direction of the stairs. What one never experienced, one never missed—wasn't that what they said? True or false, she was better off believing it.

CHAPTER FIVE

THE sun was still clear of the mainland mountain range when they emerged from the house onto the upper terrace, casting a warm glow over the faces of those still left in the courtyard. Chelsea spotted Elini, but Dion wasn't in sight.

"I saw Elini Verikiou come over to speak with you earlier," Nikos commented, following her gaze. "About what?"

"Just a friendly chat," she said, wondering why he would be interested.

"That was not the impression I received in the beginning." The hand that came under her elbow drew her back from the head of the steps she was about to start descending, turning her about to face a gaze devoid now of anything other than enquiry. "You said something to her that effected a considerable change in attitude. I want to know what you spoke of."

"Why wait till now to ask?" Chelsea prevaricated, steeling herself against the emotions his very touch still elicited.

There was irony in the line of his mouth. "I had other matters on my mind prior to this. Assuming that Dion was the subject under discussion, what did you tell Elini to put such a smile on her face?"

"The truth," she said, both unable and unwilling to come up with any further equivocation. "That she's the one he has feelings for."

No longer holding her, Nikos studied her narrowly.

"Is this something you know, or merely something you surmise?"

"It's what Dion himself told me. He was using me to arouse her jealousy."

Dark brows drew together. "You came to Skalos with him knowing it?"

"Why not?" Chelsea heard the defensive note in her voice and took steps to eradicate it. "That's what friends are for."

"Dion told *me* that the two of you met for the first time only a few days ago. A short time in which to develop the depth of friendship necessary to such a venture."

"So I'm a romantic at heart," she parried. "Anything to help the course of true love! Not that I anticipated as satisfactory an outcome, I have to admit."

"Satisfactory for whom?" Nikos looked anything but encouraging. "You believe you know Dion well enough to be sure of the permanency of these feelings he professes to have?"

Blue eyes flickered before the penetration of his gaze. She rallied with an effort. "It's obvious he's crazy about the girl."

Nikos curled a lip. "Because she resists his charms— or has done so until now. How long Dion's interest will last once she stops resisting is another matter."

Longer than Nikos's in her would last if *she* stopped resisting, Chelsea suspected. Aloud, she said stubbornly, "He won't. I'm sure of it."

"Having assured Elini of his affections, it's to be hoped you're right," came the by no means convinced response. "You will be directly responsible for any hurt she suffers."

Chelsea already knew it. Nor did the fact that she

wouldn't be around to see it if it did turn out that way
help. She'd been wrong to do what she had. Wrong to
allow herself to become involved in Dion's affairs at all.
The sooner she left the island, the better—for everyone.

Turning abruptly to start down the steps, she felt the
heel of her sandal catch on the stone edge, pitching her
forward with her ankle twisting agonisingly beneath her.
She was saved from tumbling the whole way down the
flight only by the swiftness of Nikos's reactions as he
leapt forward to seize a hold on the loose material of her
tunic and yank her backwards, inadvertently putting further strain on the twisted ankle. Chelsea felt involuntary
tears start in her eyes as pain shot up her leg.

Her cry had turned every eye in their direction. Seeing
her whitened face as he transferred his grasp from material to arm, Nikos glanced down to the foot she was
holding clear of the floor and said something short and
sharp beneath his breath. Next moment she found herself
swept up in his arms and on her way indoors again.

"I'm all right," she protested weakly, trying to ignore
the pangs. "It's only a ricked ankle. It will be fine in a
moment or two."

"It will be fine only when you can bear weight on it
without pain," he returned. "You may have broken a
bone."

If the sensations she was experiencing were anything
to go by, she had certainly suffered something more rad-
ical than a mere twist, Chelsea conceded ruefully. She
could almost feel the darned thing swelling! There had
been a weakness in that particular ankle since the time
eighteen months or so ago, when she had made a similar
misjudgement on descending a flight of steps and gone
over on it—although the pain then had been nowhere
near as bad. What she was going to do if there was a

break, she hated to think. It would certainly put paid to any further island-touring.

Nikos issued a brisk order to someone Chelsea didn't see, carrying on through a wide archway to a high-ceilinged *saloni* and depositing her on a vast and comfortable sofa.

Going down on one knee, he lifted the injured member onto a low padded stool he pulled forward, folding back the silky trouser-leg covering it to above her knee in order to have a clear view. Chelsea bit her lip in order to stop herself from crying out again as he eased the sandal from her foot, yet still found it in her to be glad that her toenails were painted a delicate pink, her skin smooth to the touch.

"You are certainly not going to walk on this!" he declared. "We can put on a compress for now, but it needs medical attention."

"You have a doctor on the island?" she asked doubtfully.

He shook his head. "One can be reached by telephone. It takes only minutes by helicopter from the mainland."

"I'm sure it isn't necessary to go to all that trouble!"

"I'll decide for myself what is necessary," came the unequivocal return as he straightened. "You will sit still while I make the call."

There was apparently no telephone in the *saloni*. Chelsea had no choice but to remain where she was as Nikos went from the room. The pain had subsided to a deep, throbbing ache, but the slightest movement still reckoned.

The same young male servant who had come to call Nikos to the telephone brought in a bowl of iced water along with a roll of crêpe bandage and a large wad of cotton wool in a wicker basket, placing them on the floor by her feet and treating her to a sympathetic glance on viewing the swollen joint.

"Doctor come soon," he assured her.

Chelsea didn't doubt it. A summons from Nikos Pandrossos would elicit instant action. What she questioned was the need for a doctor at all. The cold compress would take down the swelling, and a night's rest complete the cure—she hoped.

She took her mind off the injury by studying her surroundings. White-walled, like the rest of the house, with fine paintings and glowing Bokhara rugs supplying colour and warmth, the room was a haven. Multimillionaire though Nikos undoubtedly was, he obviously felt no desire to advertise the fact the way his aunt did. Simplicity was the keyword where his home was concerned. She could, Chelsea thought, live very happily herself in a place like this. Not that it was likely she ever would.

She pressed herself more upright on the sofa as Nikos came back into the room, catching her bottom lip between her teeth as her ankle shifted on its support.

"It's much better now," she lied. "If I rest it, it will be okay by morning, I'm sure."

"It will be for the doctor to decide that," he returned.

Chelsea watched helplessly as he dropped to one knee again to take up the wad of cotton wool and soak it in the bowl of cold water. "Couldn't one of the servants do that for me?" she protested.

The glance Nikos directed was heavy with irony. "You think I diminish myself by stooping to such a task?"

"No, of course not. I only meant—" She broke off, not at all sure quite what she *had* meant. If Nikos saw nothing untoward in what he was doing, why should she? "I'm sorry to be a nuisance," she said instead. "It was an idiotic thing to do."

"Accidents can happen to anyone," he rejoined equably, squeezing out the thick wad. "I once broke an ankle myself, skiing in the Alps."

Chelsea managed a smile. "Rather more heroic than falling down some steps!"

"The pain is the same, whichever." He applied the icy pad to the swollen area, holding it lightly in place. "We must keep doing this until the injury is cooled right down before we apply wrapping."

Eyes on the lean, long-fingered hands, pulses quickened by the contact even through the thickness of the padding, she said jerkily, "You can't stay in that position. Surely—"

"If the position irks me, I'll change it," he assured her, sounding dangerously close to irritation. "You will please stop telling me what I can or cannot do!"

Somewhat lacking during the past minutes, her sense of humour bubbled up suddenly and irrepressibly again. "Sorry," she said, adopting a meek note. "I forgot myself."

Nikos gave her an exasperated glance, dissolving into humour himself as he saw the sparkle of laughter in her eyes. "It would obviously take a great deal more than a broken ankle to subdue you for very long," he commented drily.

"I doubt very much that it's broken," she contended.

"Once again, that is for the doctor to decide. Until he does, we'll continue to treat it as a break. That means you stay where you are without further dispute."

The coldness of the compress had diminished. Nikos removed the pad and soaked it once more in the water, where ice cubes still floated, then squeezed it out to reapply, changing knees as he did so. Chelsea opened her mouth to remonstrate, then closed it again, mindful of the previous injunction.

"There can't be many women who can boast of having had Nikos Pandrossos kneeling at their feet," she quipped instead.

"No others that I recall." The dark eyes lifted to survey her, taking in every fine detail of her face beneath the mane of sun-streaked hair, his smile slow. "But then, never before have I found it desirable."

By no means blind to the deep-down burn in those eyes, Chelsea took refuge in guilelessness. "Don't you mean necessary?"

He lifted a mocking brow. "You consider me lacking in my command of your language?"

"No," she conceded. "You speak it excellently. It's just that I couldn't imagine any Greek male finding it remotely desirable to place himself in any position subservient to a woman."

The satire fired a dangerous gleam. "Subservience is a state of mind, not deed. No Greek male worthy of his manhood would allow a woman to rule him, true, but he may bend a knee to her beauty without losing face."

She was batting out of her class, Chelsea acknowledged wryly, unable to come up with a suitably flippant reply while her heart was beating hell out of her ribcage the way it was. Looking into the olive-skinned, so essentially masculine features, her ankle forgotten for the moment, she had a yearning to lean forward and take his face between her two hands, to put her lips to his in surrender to the emotions he aroused in her. He wanted her; she wanted him. What was wrong with indulging a shared desire?

Hardly practical under present circumstances, the sudden twinge reminded her. Hardly sensible under any circumstances, if it came to that. Nikos might be capable of indulging that desire with no thought beyond it, but she wasn't. It would be all too fatally easy to fall in love with him, and where would that leave her?

"You have no response for me?" he taunted.

"I was struck dumb by your eloquence," was the best she could manage.

"So it appears."

He removed the compress again and resoaked it, this time reaching for the roll of crêpe bandage after replacing the pad on the swollen area. Chelsea could only admire the dexterity with which he wrapped the bandage in the classic figure-of-eight, finishing off with a strip of tape to hold the end in place.

"The best that can be done for now," he said, getting to his feet with no sign of stiffness. "You are not to move from there!" he added sharply as she tentatively eased her foot. "Until the doctor has examined you, you will keep the ankle perfectly still."

"Your aunt will be wondering what's happening," she said. "Dion too."

As if in direct answer to the mention of his name, the latter appeared in the archway from the hall, taking in the bandaged ankle with a look of concern.

"I only just heard that you had a fall. Is it very bad?"

"We'll know that when the doctor arrives," his cousin answered before Chelsea could open her mouth.

The younger man hesitated. "How long will he be?"

"He's on the way now." Nikos added smoothly, "Break or sprain, it will be simpler if Chelsea stays here until she recovers some ease of movement. In which case, she'll need her clothing and such."

"I can't—" Chelsea began, breaking off helplessly as Nikos turned a quelling glance on her.

"There's no reason to transport you across the island when facilities are available here. Dion will go now and collect your things."

It was obvious from the latter's face that he resented the order, but he made no attempt to dispute it, turning without another word and vanishing the way he had come. What Nikos said went, Chelsea gathered. She knew the feeling.

There was no actual need for her to stay right here, of course. Even if she couldn't put her foot to the ground, it would be simple enough to get her out to the car. Kiria Pandrossos might not be too pleased to have an invalid on her hands, but, having already noted the interest taken in her erstwhile guest by the man she coveted as a son-in-law, she would probably rather put up with that than leave her in his care.

None of which made any difference whatsoever, of course. Nikos had decided, therefore here she would stay. It was the possible ulterior motive that bothered her the most. A sprained ankle—and she was certain it amounted to no more than that—was no barrier to love-making, which he certainly did have in mind where she was concerned. It might even be called an asset, she reflected, in the sense that it stopped her from running away.

"If you're afraid that I may take advantage of your disability, you needn't be," Nikos commented, reading her without effort. "When we come together, it will be with your total compliance, I assure you."

"Does the word 'if' figure in your vocabulary at all?" she queried on a tart note, gathering herself.

"*If* implies doubt, and we both know the inevitability

of what is to happen between us," came the unmoved response. "We were fated to meet, you and I."

She was wasting her breath, Chelsea acknowledged wryly. His assurance was beyond deflation by mere words. If he meant what he said about compliance, then the ball was in her court.

Which was hardly a reassuring thought, considering how rarely she held her own at that game either.

The noise that had slowly impinged on her consciousness in the past few seconds resolved itself into the unmistakable clattering sound of a helicopter. Coming in to land on one of the lower levels, she judged.

Nikos moved to the nearest window to watch the aircraft, blocking out much of the remaining light with his breadth of shoulder.

"It's going to be dark before long," Chelsea ventured. "Will it be able to get off again?"

"With the pad floodlit, there won't be any difficulty," he said. "The pilots are accustomed to both day and night flying."

"Does that mean you use helicopters yourself for transportation sometimes?"

"When time is pressing, yes."

"But you don't keep one here on the island?"

"Maintenance is easier on the mainland, and it takes no more than fifteen minutes to have one fly out."

Plus having one sitting out there all the time wouldn't exactly enhance the scene, Chelsea agreed, assuming that factor had some bearing too. Nikos would obviously far prefer to use other, less intrusive forms of transport, like the yacht she had seen sitting out in the bay.

She'd never been sailing herself. It must, she thought, be an exhilarating experience to skim over the water, the sails billowing in the wind and the taste of salt on one's lips. Even more so with Nikos at the helm. A somewhat cynical friend of hers had once said that men referred to both boats and cars in the feminine because they liked to believe they could handle women with equal skill. While that might not be true of a lot, with Nikos...

She came down to earth with a bump as a small, swarthy man came through the archway. He was carrying a battered leather bag of the type used by medics the world over, though, wearing trousers and casual shirt, and badly in need of a shave, he looked far from the distinguished, impeccably clad character she had somehow expected to see.

Nikos greeted him in Greek, and brought the man over to where to where Chelsea sat waiting, introducing him as Dr Kalvos.

Whatever her reservations regarding his appearance, he certainly seemed to know his job. She tensed as he examined the site of injury after removing the bandage, but his blunt-fingered hands were unexpectedly gentle in their touch.

"I think no bones broken," he declared at length. "But there must be no weight put upon the limb until the swelling has decreased, when I will examine it once more. Until then, it must remain supported."

"It will," Nikos assured him, cutting across what Chelsea was about to say.

He lapsed into Greek again when he accompanied the doctor out, disappearing for only a moment or two before returning to view her expression with lifted brows.

"I told you it was only a sprain," she burst out. "There was no cause to bring him haring all the way over! Supposing someone had really needed him?"

"He would have been summoned. And there was

cause enough,'' Nikos said firmly. "He said you may take aspirin for the pain.''

"I don't need painkillers,'' she asserted. "It doesn't hurt any more. I could easily—'' She winced as she made an involuntary movement, and saw his derisive smile.

"You could easily do little. The good doctor will return in two days. Until then...'' He paused with deliberation, eyes acquiring a devilish glint. "Until then, you are at my mercy, *agapi mou*.''

"Don't count on it,'' she said weakly.

"But I do count on it.''

He set a knee on the sofa at her side, one hand sliding over the back to hold himself steady, the other down her cheek to turn her face towards him. The kiss was infinitely light, lips just brushing hers at first, then gently teasing them apart. The silky touch of his tongue sent her pulse-rate through the roof. She responded blindly, hands lifting of their own accord to seek the breadth of his chest, fingers curling into muscle-etched flesh—helpless against the tidal wave of passion sweeping over her.

"You see,'' Nikos said softly, lifting his head at last. "You can refuse me nothing.''

"You can lead a horse to water...'' she murmured unsteadily.

He gave a low laugh. "If by that you mean that it will drink only if thirsty, then I'd say that the point has already been made. You hunger for me the same way I hunger for you, and our appetites must be assuaged.''

How was it, thought Chelsea in some bemusement, that what would sound simply soppy on an Englishman's lips could take on such different connotations? If Nikos found it easy to speak this way now, what might he be moved to come out with in the throes of passion?

"Your guests will be wondering where you got to," she said, cutting off that line of reflection. "It must be an hour or more since you carried me in here."

"Most will have left by now," came the untroubled reply. "The rest will be taken care of." He eased himself upright without kissing her again, to her mingled relief and disappointment. "The room I ordered prepared for you will be ready by now. I think I should take you there, and allow you to rest. Your things will be brought to you when Dion returns with them."

He suited his actions to his words, bending to sweep her up from the sofa into his arms again while taking care not to jolt her ankle. Chelsea resisted with an effort the urge to lay her head against the broad shoulder, holding herself stiffly as he carried her through to the hall.

Apart from a solitary member of staff, who happened to be crossing the hall, there was no one in sight. Chelsea was thankful for that. The last thing she needed was an audience.

"Relax," Nikos admonished on a dry note, setting foot on the stairs. "I'm not about to drop you."

Chelsea could well believe it. Her hundred and twenty pounds appeared to be causing him no problem at all. She did her best to loosen up, but with her every nerve-ending quivering to the feel of him, it was a very poor best.

The bedroom he took her to was at the rear of the house, with double glass doors opening onto a balcony and what in daylight would be a magnificent sea view. As on the floor below, the furnishings were of excellent quality but without ostentation, the colours muted. Nikos set her down on the double bed, straightening to eye her quizzically as she geared herself for his next move.

"Your injury must take precedence over other needs

for the present,'' he said. ''By the time I return from Athens—''

''You're leaving Skalos!''

His slow smile took due note of the perturbation she couldn't conceal. ''For three days only—perhaps even less.''

''On business?''

''No other cause would draw me from your side!''

Not *this* side of fulfilling his desires, at any rate, came the passing thought.

''I can't stay here if you're not going to be here yourself,'' she protested.

The smile widened. ''I'm delighted that my absence matters so much to you.''

''That wasn't what I meant.''

''Yes, it was. We'll both of us be counting the minutes until we can be together. And until that time,'' Nikos continued, before she could form a riposte to that piece of extravagance, ''you are not to set your foot to the floor. Ledra will extend her duties to help you where necessary, and your meals will be brought to you. That way we can be sure you do no further damage.''

Blue eyes sparked. ''If you think I'm going to spend three whole days sitting here twiddling my thumbs—''

''Doctor's orders. As to entertainment, I'll arrange for reading matter in English to be brought to you, so your thumbs may remain idle.''

Chelsea regarded him helplessly. She had never been in a situation she hadn't been able to control before, and didn't much care for the feeling now.

''Your solicitude does you credit,'' was all she was able to come up with.

''Does it not?'' he agreed imperturbably. ''Dion should have returned by now, I think.''

Don't go, she almost blurted out as he started to turn away, biting it back just in time. So far as tonight went she was obviously stuck with the situation, but tomorrow was another story. There was no way she was going to just sit around waiting for him. *No* way!

CHAPTER SIX

WOKEN by the sound of the helicopter coming in to land, Chelsea knew a momentary disorientation before memory kicked in. She moved her foot tentatively, grimacing as pain speared through her ankle. If it felt like that now, she certainly wasn't going to be able to walk on it. Today, at any rate.

It wasn't yet seven o'clock, she saw, reaching for the watch she had left on the bedside table. Nikos obviously planned to get to where he was going early.

She had seen neither him nor Dion again last night. Along with her baggage had been delivered a wheelchair, procured from God only knew where. It stood now at the side of the bed, where she could ease herself into it in order to reach the bathroom right next door. The same one she had used on her previous foray, which meant she was just across the corridor from Dimitris's room. Hopefully, she would be seeing something of the child. Unlike his father, he presented no problems.

A tap on the door heralded the entry of the woman who had given her assistance in preparing for bed last night. In her mid-thirties, at a guess, and wearing dark clothing that did nothing to enhance her somewhat severe looks, Ledra was far from the kind of nanny Chelsea would have deemed suitable for a child Dimitris's age and character. She spoke little English, but still managed to make it more than apparent that she resented the task allocated to her.

"Kalimera," she responded shortly to Chelsea's overture. "You want help?"

Already sitting up, Chelsea summoned a smile, shaking her head. *"Ochi, efcharisto.* I can manage."

The older woman shrugged and turned to leave, falling back in some confusion as her employer appeared in the open doorway. Wearing a superbly cut lightweight suit in pale beige, his deeper toned shirt open on the taut column of his throat, he looked devastating. Chelsea put up an automatic hand to smooth her bed-tumbled hair as she met the dark eyes, wondering what on earth *she* must look like.

"You might have waited till I was dressed!" she exclaimed, feeling more than a little vulnerable in the flimsy nightdress that left her shoulders and a not inconsiderable portion of cleavage on view.

"No time," he returned equably.

He added something in Greek to the nurse, prompting her immediate withdrawal from the room, and advanced further into it himself. Amusement creased the corners of mouth and eyes at Chelsea's involuntary move to pull up the sheet she had thrust back preparatory to easing herself out to the chair.

"A tantalising glimpse of the delights I look forward to savouring in full on my return," he said.

"You're taking a hell of a lot for granted!" she retorted, and saw the amusement deepen.

"I think not. In three days' time, if your ankle is healed, we set the seal on our relationship. It will be a turbulent one, I fancy."

Her brows drew together. "Relationship?"

"But of course. Did you imagine I'd want only the one time with you?"

"Did *you* imagine I'd consent to more?" she shot

back, only realising what she was implying when it was too late to rephrase. ''That wasn't what I meant,'' she hastened to add.

''So you keep telling me.'' The devilish spark was there in his eyes. ''What is the slang term the English sometimes use to express the difference between the word and the thought?''

''Paying lip service'' was what he had in mind, Chelsea surmised. Not all that far off the mark, although she had no intention of admitting it.

''I'm not about to become a plaything, for you or anyone else,'' she declared with force. ''So forget it! The minute I can put one foot in front of the other, I'm out of here!''

''How would you propose to leave?'' Nikos asked calmly.

''Dion—'' she began, breaking off as he shook his head.

''Dion won't be available.''

Chelsea ran a fraught hand through her hair, oblivious now to however she might look. ''You can't keep me here against my will!''

''I wouldn't attempt to do so. Providing all goes well, your ankle should be sufficiently recovered by the time I return for the decision to be made one way or the other.'' He paused, gaze roving her finely moulded features and semi-clad upper body with a certain deliberation. ''For now, however...''

She eyed him with mixed emotions as he came towards the bed, not at all certain that he didn't intend taking full advantage of her helplessness here and now.

''Hold it right there!'' she commanded, trying to sound as if she really meant it when every instinct in her was urging the direct opposite.

For all the notice he took, she might as well have saved her breath. Sitting down on the edge of the bed, he drew her unresistingly to him. The kiss was gentle, lulling her into a sense of false security in its very lack of demand. She barely felt the touch of his hands on her shoulders, becoming aware of his intention only when he slid both narrow straps downwards to bare her breasts. Even then she made no move to stop him, wanting—yearning—aching for his caresses.

He murmured something thickly beneath his breath, and bent to take one tingling, peaking nipple between his lips, sliding his tongue over and around the proud nub until she could barely stand the sensation. It was a jolt to her whole system when he put her firmly from him.

"I must go," he said, regret in both eyes and voice. "Anything you need, you have only to ask for."

The only thing she needed right now was a continuation of what had just gone, Chelsea thought wryly. So much for all her brave talk! She pulled up her nightdress straps with nerveless fingers as Nikos got to his feet, unable to look him in the eye.

"I'll be back as soon as is possible," he said softly. *"Kali andomosi, agapi mou."*

He went without looking back, leaving the door ajar. Chelsea heard him say something, and then a childish voice answering. A moment later, a pyjama-clad Dimitris appeared in the doorway, viewing her with heartwarming delight.

"Papa says you are to stay!" he exclaimed, adding as an afterthought, "I'm sorry you are hurt."

"It's nothing much," Chelsea assured him. "I'll be as fit as a flea in a day or two."

The boy giggled. "Fleas are not nice!"

Considering his surroundings, Chelsea doubted if he had ever actually seen one. "No, they're not," she agreed. "But they can jump, while I can't even walk at present."

"Is that why you have a chair on wheels?" he asked, eyes lighting on the vehicle. "I could push you."

"I think you'd better go and get dressed first," she said diplomatically as Ledra loomed behind him. "If you want to come back and visit after breakfast, I'd love to see you."

"I will," he promised.

Nikos must have been spotted making his way down to the landing pad, Chelsea surmised, hearing the helicopter start up again as the boy disappeared. If she could make it across to the balcony, she could see it take off.

It wasn't too difficult getting out of the bed and into the chair, having already had practice at it last night, and there was plenty of room to manoeuvre. The balcony doors were covered on the outside by slatted shutters, one pair opening inwards and the other outwards, which didn't make manipulation easy. By the time she emerged onto the balcony, the machine was already rising.

Both pilot and passenger were plainly in view. Only when the latter turned his head to look directly at her did Chelsea remember her scanty apparel, thankful that the pilot was too busy with the controls to spare a glance himself. Nikos lifted a hand in mocking farewell as the machine hovered for a brief moment before swinging away.

The yellow and white craft was a mere dot in the sky when Chelsea finally turned her attention to the magnificent scenery. From this height, she could see down over all three levels to the outer rim of a white curve of beach bounded either side by low cliffs. Too small a cove to harbour a yacht the size of the one she had seen on arrival, she guessed, although there was a smaller craft riding at anchor a little way out. The sea was a vast blue spread, sparkling in the sunlight.

It was going to be a frustrating few days in more ways than one, she thought ruefully. Had she been fit, she could at least have spent the time exploring.

On the other hand, if she were fit she wouldn't be here at all, she reminded herself.

What exactly Nikos had in mind when he spoke of a relationship, she wasn't at all sure. More than a one-night stand, for certain, but how much more? A few days? A week or two? It would depend, she supposed, on how long she could keep his interest from flagging.

She pulled herself up there, shocked by the route her thoughts were taking. Mistress of a Greek tycoon, that was what she was actually contemplating becoming. Not the first he'd had, if she was any judge at all. Maybe not even the only one in present running. For all she knew, he had mistresses all over the place!

The wisest course she could take was to be gone before he got back. Dion might have been told not to transport her, but there had to be other ways of getting off the island. Once she could hobble…

She made a wry grimace, forced to admit that she couldn't bear the thought of leaving. Nikos only had to look at her to turn her knees to jelly, only had to touch her to have her quivering like an aspen leaf in a gale. To spend a whole night in his arms would be out of this world!

So why not make it just the one? He had already said he wouldn't attempt to keep her here against her will. She closed heart and mind against the deep-down knowledge that once would not be enough—that Nikos Pandrossos would be all too easy a man to fall in love with.

The day went through its phases, with meals brought to her on a tray by Ledra. The latter put up no objection to Dimitris spending time with her in the afternoon. She probably, Chelsea thought, welcomed the opportunity to visit with her gardener friend.

She found it difficult to imagine that their friendship could be anything but platonic. The possibility that beneath the dour exterior might lurk a full-blooded, needful woman seemed remote. Recalling Nikos's view of male/female relationships, she doubted if he would approve of the association all the same. Not when the woman was supposed to be looking after his son.

So far as Chelsea herself was concerned, having the child around was a pleasure. Under his expert tuition, she became quite proficient with the pinball machine, gaining kudos on her own behalf by introducing him to paper and pencil games dredged up from memory. He absolutely adored her version of Hangman, chuckling with glee when he guessed a correct letter and was able to add another detail to his matchstick figure. They played in English, of course, using simple words at first. But Chelsea found herself forced to increase the difficulty in order to have any chance of winning. The extent of his vocabulary constantly amazed her.

He showed a will to equal his father's when Ledra finally came to take him away. Only when told he could come back again the next day did he reluctantly concede. Chelsea wondered if the woman ever played with him at all. On the face of it, it seemed doubtful. Perhaps she didn't consider games an essential part of her duties. Whatever, she was far from the mother substitute an ideal nanny should surely be.

Left alone, with the evening stretching into infinity, she attempted to read one of the books brought to her, but could find no interest in it. Inevitably her thoughts turned to the master of the house, wondering what he was doing right now. For certain there would be female company available if he wanted it. Nice as it was to imagine that he might forgo the pleasure in consideration of his interest in herself, she very much doubted it. For a man such as Nikos sexual fulfilment was like breathing—essential to life. What she still had to decide was just how essential it was to her.

Morning saw a distinct improvement in the state of her ankle. She could move her foot without very much pain at all now, and walk on it too, providing she didn't bring her full weight to bear. No break, for certain. Not even a bad sprain if it healed this quickly, although the swelling had certainly been real enough.

Could the subconscious, Chelsea wondered, actually conjure up physical symptoms? There was no doubt that she'd wanted to stay on. What she'd lacked was the courage to do it regardless. A cynic might suggest that the fall itself had been self-induced.

It was a real disappointment when Dimitris failed to put in an appearance after breakfast. By ten o'clock, Chelsea could bear the solitude no longer. Wearing white cotton shorts and sleeveless top, with a pair of trainers on her feet to lend extra support, she made a slow but sure passage along the corridor and down the stairs.

There was neither sight nor sound of Dimitris. Ledra had taken him to the beach, she managed to glean from a member of staff she came across on the patio. It was a fair way down, via many steps, and a foolhardy thing to do in her condition, but she went anyway. Dimitris apart, a paddle in salt water could do nothing but good.

With rails to hold onto for support, the descent proved easy enough, although her ankle was hurting for real by the time she reached the final stage. She'd be fine after a rest, Chelsea reassured herself, reluctant to admit that she shouldn't have tried it.

She was nonplussed to find the curve of beach apparently empty of human occupation. Perhaps they'd gone out to the boat, she thought, shading her eyes with the back of her hand as she peered across the sun-sparkled water. Unable to see any movement on board the cabin cruiser, she brought her attention back to dry land, only then spotting the dinghy moored to a small landing stage further along the beach. Not that, then, so...

Looking seawards again, her gaze was caught and held by what looked from this distance like a small bundle of rags rolling in the gentle waves. Even as she focused she was moving, kicking off her trainers as she went and oblivious to the pain that shot up her leg as she ran across the sand to plunge through the shallows and launch into a fast crawl.

Dimitris was unconscious when she reached him, a limp little figure in the red shirt that had caught her eye, the beach ball bobbing nearby mute testimony. Chelsea could feel a faint pulse, but he had stopped breathing. She began resuscitation right there in the water, covering both mouth and nostrils with her lips and giving two exhalations before turning on her back with the small body firmly supported to kick out strongly for the shore.

The moment her feet touched bottom, she stood up thigh-deep and recommenced the mouth-to-mouth, willing the child to respond, to cough up the water he must have swallowed and begin breathing for himself again.

She was vaguely aware of figures on the beach, and could hear a wailing sound, as of someone in dire distress, but it was all on the periphery. Only when the small chest suddenly heaved of its own accord, and then convulsed in a paroxysm of coughing, did she stumble out of the water, fiercely avoiding the rush Ledra made to snatch the little body from her arms.

"Get help!" she yelled at the woman. *"Yatros!"*

Dimitris was crying now, hiccuping water and mucus between sobs, his arms wrapped tight about Chelsea's neck. With no idea how long he had been in the water, there was no certainty yet that he hadn't suffered brain damage, but she didn't think so. His eyes were open, and looked focused through the tears.

Ledra made no move to obey the command, dancing from foot to foot in wild-eyed agitation as she poured out a stream of Greek Chelsea didn't stand a cat in hell's chance of understanding. The man who had been there too had disappeared, whether to do what Ledra was refusing to do or simply to put distance between him and disaster Chelsea didn't know, and couldn't afford to care right now. Hoisting the child more firmly in her arms, she started for the steps, ignoring the pain from her ankle.

How she made it to the top, barefoot and unable to seek support from the guardrail, she never knew. By the time she reached the courtyard she was past feeling anything. A man and a girl came running, jabbering in consternation as they assessed the situation. The girl darted off, hopefully to call for the doctor Chelsea considered vital to the child's well being, even if he was on the way to recovery. She refused the man's attempt to take the boy from her, making for the house with him running agitatedly alongside.

Dimitris had stopped crying some time ago, and looked on the verge of sleep when she reached his room. Chelsea stripped off his wet clothing and wrapped him in thick dry towels, accepting another from the young male servant who had followed her to wrap around her own dripping hair. With the child settled in bed and exhaustedly asleep, there was little else to be done except wait for the doctor to arrive.

Leaving the boy supervised, she went to change her clothing. Reaction was setting in, trembling her limbs and turning her stomach inside out. Her face in the mirror looked pinched, her eyes bruised. There were red marks on her neck where small hands had clutched her.

Her ankle had swelled again, the bandage long gone. Sitting on the bath-edge, with her foot supported on a stool, Chelsea laid cold wet flannels over the area. Her trainers were still down on the beach, for what it mattered: she wasn't going to be able to get them on again for a while anyway. A pair of sandals would have to suffice for now.

Dressed in one of her long Indian cotton skirts and a cool tie top, she briefly contemplated using the wheelchair again, but deemed it more trouble than it was worth. She found Dimitris still asleep, and breathing quite normally, curly dark head just about dry.

Chelsea indicated to the young man still watching over him to fetch another pillow, and exchanged it for the damp one without waking the boy. He looked so small, so defenceless lying there. She wanted to pick him up and hug him to her.

The same doctor who had attended her arrived some minutes later. He woke Dimitris in order to ascertain his condition throughout, then allowed him to go back to sleep again.

"All appears well," he declared. "You saved both his life and his brain, *despinis*. Kirios Pandrossos will be for ever in your debt!"

Chelsea shook her head. "It's enough that he's going to be all right. Kirios Pandrossos has had enough tragedy in his life." She added hesitantly, "He's in Athens right now. Do you think he should be informed?"

"I am told it has been done already," the doctor returned. "The nurse will face his wrath for her neglect— if she dares stay to do so. To fall asleep on a beach when in charge of a small child is a terrible thing!"

Recalling the man who had been there too, Chelsea doubted if sleep had been the cause of the woman's distraction. The two of them must have gone in among the rocks, leaving the child to play alone while they indulged themselves.

"Yes, it is," she said, aware that she owed it to Nikos to put him fully in the picture, but reluctant to discuss the subject with anyone else. "The woman deserves to lose her job."

The doctor glanced down at her ankle as she shifted uncomfortably, brows drawing together. "You must allow me to examine your injury again. There appears to be even more swelling than there was before."

"Just too much use too soon, I suppose," Chelsea responded lightly. "It will go down again."

"Not unless you do as you are told and rest," came the severe retort, softened by a sudden smile. "Although it was fortunate for Dimitris that you disobeyed today."

Wasn't it, though? Chelsea thought thankfully. It was worth any amount of pain to have him safe!

Confined to the wheelchair again, after the doctor had immobilised her ankle in bandages once more and left, she insisted on returning to Dimitris's room to keep an eye on the sleeping child. Where Ledra was she had no idea. It was possible, she supposed, that the woman had taken flight in fear of retribution. Nikos was hardly going to look leniently on the betrayal of trust—especially when he knew the full story.

Chelsea smothered any inclination towards sympathy for the woman. She merited none.

She dozed on and off herself during the following hour or so, though with an ear cocked for any sound from the bed. When Dimitris did finally awake he showed no physical ill-effects, though it was more than possible, Chelsea reflected, that he would be wary of the sea for a while.

He'd been trying to reach his ball, which had floated away, he told her. He had tried to swim, as his father had showed him, but he'd swallowed some water and then the sun had disappeared.

"I called for Ledra, but she had gone to talk with Stavros," he said. "Where is she now?"

"I don't know," Chelsea admitted. "Are you hungry?"

The dark eyes brightened. "*Ne!* I mean, yes."

"It's all right," she assured him smilingly. "I can understand simple words."

Up on his knees now, looking totally recovered, he said eagerly, "I will tell you more words if you will be my nurse instead of Ledra!"

Chelsea hardly knew how to reply to that. She copped out by murmuring something about it being his father's place to decide such matters, following with a hasty query as to what he fancied to eat. Judging from his reaction to the question, he wasn't normally given a choice, but he lost little time in taking advantage of the offer. Chelsea could only hope that pizza was going to be available in *this* Greek homestead.

It was, it turned out, not only available but ready to eat in less than twenty minutes. She had the same herself, mainly because she couldn't think of anything else she fancied, and enjoyed every crumb. Dimitris's room didn't have a balcony, so they had the meal served on hers, along with tall, frosted glasses of fruit juice.

They were still out there when the helicopter returned. Nikos came up the steps with speed and agility, pausing on the patio to look up at the two of them with a grim expression that lightened only fractionally when his son waved an eager arm.

Chelsea turned her chair to face the balcony doorway in preparation for his appearance, thankful that it was Ledra and not herself who was responsible for the near calamity. So far there was no sign of the woman. Unless she had some private means of leaving the island, she had to be somewhere around, but obviously reluctant to face up to her misdeeds. For that, Chelsea couldn't blame her. She had a feeling that Nikos would know no mercy.

CHAPTER SEVEN

HE WAS in total control of his emotions by the time he appeared in the doorway, able to return his son's light-hearted greeting in similar vein. Yesterday's suit had been replaced by one of rather more sober cut and hue, subtly fining down the broad-shouldered outline.

"I have no appetite," he said, declining Dimitris's invitation to sample the pizza still remaining. "Perhaps you should go now and wash away the traces of yours before the flies begin to think you a buffet table for their especial use!"

Chuckling at the idea, the boy did as he was bid. Only when he was clear of the room did Nikos step out onto the balcony, to sink into the chair his son had vacated with an exhalation that registered an inner release.

"I was in a meeting when the call came," he said. "Until the moment I saw the two of you sitting here, I couldn't be sure all was well again." The dark eyes held an expression that caused Chelsea's heart to palpitate. "I owe you more than I can ever repay."

"You owe me nothing," she said huskily. "I just happened to be there at the right time, that's all."

"But how?" he demanded, viewing the wrapped and obviously swollen ankle.

"It wasn't like this earlier," she said. "It only swelled up again after I got back up the steps."

"Carrying my son." He inclined his head as she looked her surprise. "Dr Kalvos contacted me on the mobile telephone. He said you refused to allow anyone to take Dimitris from you, even though in pain. That you insisted on staying with him in your wet clothing until you could be certain of his well being.''

"I'd more or less dried off by the time we reached the house,'' Chelsea said self-deprecatingly, wishing he would stop. "Anyway, all's well that ends well.''

"Except that it is far from ended.'' The grimness was back in both face and voice. "I understand that Ledra hasn't been seen since the incident.''

"No.'' Chelsea hesitated, torn between two fires. Nikos had a right to know the truth, yet it still felt like telling tales out of school. "She was with Stavros,'' she said. "Not for the first time, I believe.''

The dark brows drew together. "Stavros?''

"One of the gardeners. At least, that's what Dimitris told me.''

Nikos was sitting up straighter in the chair, eyes narrowed to gleaming jet points. "Dimitris *knew* of this...liaison?''

"He knew she visited the man. I doubt if he realised the reason. If it comes to that,'' she added, trying to be fair, "*I* can't say for certain that they were doing anything they shouldn't. They weren't in sight when I got to the beach.''

"I would say there was no doubt at all.'' The very tone sent a shiver down Chelsea's back. "They will both pay dearly for their violation!''

They had to be found first, it was on the tip of her tongue to say, but she bit it back. If Nikos Pandrossos wanted them found, found they would be.

The helicopter had not taken straight off again. She said tentatively, "Will you be going back to Athens?''

He shook his head. "Not immediately. Negotiations can continue without me.''

As if in direct response, the helicopter engine started up. Chelsea watched the machine rise and swing away with lightened heart, looking back to find Nikos watching her, an enigmatic expression in his eyes.

"I find myself in something of a dilemma," he said. "Dimitris has need of a new nurse, but it will be difficult to find one I can trust after Ledra proved herself so much less than her references led me to believe. Perhaps you'd consider taking up the position yourself in the meantime?"

Chelsea gazed at him in silence for a lengthy moment, mind grappling with the connotations. He was offering her a job, albeit a temporary one, but how could that fit in with his professed interest in her as a woman?

The answer was simple: it couldn't. Dimitris's safety meant more to him than any sexual desire. She supposed she should feel gratified that he was willing to put his trust in her, but all she could feel right now was a sense of loss.

"You don't know me," she pointed out, trying to sound practical about it. "How can you be sure I'm the right kind of person to look after your son?"

"Because you already proved it by doing as you did this morning. Because Dimitris is happy to be with you." There was determination in every line of the hard-boned face. "You said the other evening that you were of independent means, and with no demands on your time. One month is all I ask. I have no one else to put faith in."

Chelsea drew in a long, slow breath, fighting to stay on top of her warring emotions. "There's always Florina. I'm sure she'd be only too willing to—"

"I've no intention of asking Florina," came the unequivocal response. "I'm asking *you!* The salary—"

"Don't insult me!" Chelsea found release in anger, eyes striking blue sparks. "Do you think I'd take money for merely keeping an eye on a five-year-old child?"

"There's far more to the job than that, as you well know," Nikos returned levelly. "I meant no insult." He paused, expression unreadable now. "If you won't take on the task in any formal capacity, perhaps you'd consider it as a personal favour to me?"

Chelsea bit her lip, aware of being put in a cleft stick. If she refused she would in effect be saying that Dimitris's welfare wasn't important to her, yet to go along with the request meant accepting a situation where her own needs and desires would have to be sublimated. Nikos could accept that, because his feelings towards her were purely physical and therefore of no particular consequence, whereas hers towards him...

She shut off the thought before it reached a conclusion, summoning a smile and a light shrug.

"Put that way, how can I say no?"

The strong features relaxed. "You have my gratitude in this too. You must regard yourself as family while you're here. Everything I own is at your disposal."

"I'll need to phone *my* family to let them know where I'll be for the next few weeks," she said, wondering how her mother in particular was going to react to the news. Better, despite her professed modernistic attitude to life, than if she admitted her less worthy inclinations, for sure.

"Of course. Unfortunately there's no telephone in this room, but you can use the one in my bedroom, which is only two doors away." Nikos got to his feet. "I'll take you there now."

Making sure she didn't change her mind, Chelsea surmised as he moved behind her to reach the chair handles.

Not that he need worry about that. For the next month, Dimitris had to be her sole concern.

The master bedroom proved no larger and no more sumptuously furnished than her own. What it lacked was any hint of the feminine touch—surfaces clear of everything bar essentials. The telephone was on the bedside table. Nikos wheeled the chair over and set it where she could easily reach the instrument, putting on the brake.

"You'd like me to speak to your parents myself?" he asked.

Chelsea hastily shook her head. "That's all right. It's just a case of explaining the change in plan, so that they won't be looking for any more postcards."

"Ah, yes, I was forgetting. They have no authority over your movements."

"Not in the sense of my having to ask permission to take the job on, no," she agreed, sensing irony.

The dark eyes acquired an indefinable expression. "Not a job," he reminded her. "A favour. Unless, of course, you'd like to reconsider the terms?"

"Of course not." Chelsea could say that much with certainty. "I look forward to spending time with Dimitris. He's a super child altogether."

Nikos inclined his head. "Thank you. I think so too, of course—although he can misbehave at times."

"Children who never misbehave are probably too cowed to think of it. I doubt if he could think up any more mischief than the average five-year-old—including myself, if my mother is to be believed," she tagged on humorously. "According to her, I was born wayward!"

"If that means the same as wilful, I'd say there has been little change." The accompanying smile robbed the words of any sting. "It would have been difficult, I'm sure, to discipline the adorable, golden-haired sprite you must have been. Especially when you widened those blue eyes so innocently, the way you do with me still.''

Standing there, close enough that she had to crick her neck to look up at him, his shirt collar opened on a glimpse of black hair, he had the blood coursing through her veins like hot oil. "I never," she protested weakly, and saw the smile slowly widen.

"You're doing it now. An irresistible enticement!"

Chelsea made an involuntary and, because of the brake, futile attempt to back up the chair as he bent to run both hands into the soft thickness of her hair and tilt her head to receive his lips. The kiss was like nothing that had gone before—a mingling of tenderness and controlled passion that set her alight. It lasted all too brief a time, and left her quivering with suppressed emotion. She couldn't find a single thing to say when Nikos straightened again.

"Now telephone your parents," he instructed. "I'll go and tell Dimitris the good news."

He was at the door before Chelsea found her voice. She was unsurprised to hear the unsteadiness. "Am I to understand that my working for you makes no difference to our...relationship?"

"*If* you worked for me, it might," he returned equably. "The payment could be misconstrued. As it is, I see no reason for either of us to deny our needs."

You're taking an awful lot for granted again! she wanted to fling after him as he departed, except that he wasn't, of course. He knew exactly what had been going through her mind these last minutes. He'd probably counted on her refusing to accept payment for looking after his son.

There was no future in it, the small voice of reason warned her. One short month, that was all he was asking of her. She could refuse to meet him on that level, of course. He would accept it for Dimitris's sake if she made an issue of it.

Only she wouldn't, she knew. She didn't have sufficient strength of mind to withstand the way Nikos made her feel. A month of knowing him the way she yearned to know him was better than a lifetime of wondering what she might have missed. One month. Thirty days— and nights. He wouldn't be here for all of them, of course, but when he was...

The telephone! she told herself severely, shelving the thought for later.

The call went through without delay. Hardly surprising considering Nikos's need to be in easy touch with his business interests both in and out of Greece. Mobiles weren't always the most reliable of instruments.

Her mother answered on the third ring, surprised to hear her voice on the line.

"I thought where you planned on going the telephone wouldn't even be installed yet!" she commented. "Which island are you on right now? You sound right next door!"

"It's called Skalos," Chelsea told her.

"Skalos? I don't think I ever heard of it."

"It's doubtful if you would have. It's privately owned."

"Really?" The interest deepened. "Who by?"

"The Pandrossos Shipping Company, to be exact."

"Now, *that* I've certainly heard of! How on earth did you manage to manoeuvre yourself into those circles?"

"It's a long story." Chelsea had no intention of going into detail. "The thing is, I shan't be moving around the way I intended. I'm looking after the company president's young son for the next few weeks, until someone trustworthy is found to take over.''

''This is a first, even for you!'' Her mother sounded more than a little bemused. ''What qualifications do you have as a nanny?''

Chelsea gave a laugh. ''Compared with Briony's two, Dimitris will be a doddle! Anyway, it's only a month.''

''Supposing they don't find anyone? Will the mother be prepared to take over from you?''

''He doesn't have a mother. She was killed when he was a toddler.'' Chelsea took care to keep her tone neutral. ''Kirios Pandrossos is away on business a lot, hence the need for a nanny.''

''Poor man!'' There was a slight pause. ''How old is he?''

''I'm not sure,'' Chelsea hedged. ''Mid-thirties, I suppose.''

''That's very young to be in his position, isn't it?''

''I wouldn't know. It could be the norm here.'' Time to curtail this before her mother's curiosity was whetted any further, Chelsea decided. ''I have to go,'' she said. ''I'll ring again in a few days. Love to all.''

She rang off before any further comment could be made, and sat for a moment contemplating the question of just what *was* going to happen if no suitable replacement for Ledra could be found inside the month. It wasn't outside the bounds of possibility—even probability—that Nikos would have exhausted his passion for her by then. Even if he hadn't, the longer she indulged hers for him the harder it would be to cut loose.

Live for today, not tomorrow, she told herself resolutely. Whatever happened, she would handle it.

Dimitris erupted through the doorway as if shot from

a gun, launching himself onto her lap to throw both arms about her neck and submit her to a fierce hug.

"Papa says you're to be my new nurse!" he said excitedly. "Can we play the Hangman game again?"

Chelsea hugged the small wiry body back, laughing at the child's order of priorities. "It's supposed to be siesta time."

"I think we can forgo that for today," said Nikos from the door. "Calm yourself, Dimitris, and get down from there. Chelsea is still in pain from her ankle."

"Not very much," she denied as the child slid obediently back to the ground. "In fact, I don't really need the chair at all."

"You'll stay in it the rest of the day at least," Nikos responded firmly. "The doctor will say if you can discard it when he visits again in the morning."

Blue eyes widened with deliberation. *"Yes, sir!"*

The strong mouth took on a slant. "That's better. I will have obedience from my subordinates!"

"Will you play Hangman too?" asked Dimitris hopefully, before Chelsea could come up with a suitably diluted retort. "I can show you how."

His father lifted his shoulders in tolerant resignation. "Allow me a few minutes to change my clothing first."

"We'll be out on my balcony," Chelsea told him, releasing the brake in order to turn the chair about. "If I have to stay up here, I can at least do it in the fresh air."

"I'll have someone come to draw down the canopy," Nikos answered as she headed for the door with Dimitris trundling happily alongside. "None but the English would sit out in the full heat of the afternoon sun!"

"You're forgetting mad dogs," she tossed over a

shoulder, eliciting a gurgle of laughter from the diminutive figure at her side.

Almost before they had reached the balcony themselves, the same young man who had accompanied her up from the courtyard with Dimitris earlier arrived to pull down the canopy she hadn't even known was there. Nikos must, Chelsea reflected, have some form of intercom connected to his room to have got things moving so fast. She had to admit that it was far more comfortable in the shade. Safer too, considering the strength of the sun in this part of the world.

Dimitris went and found another pencil to add to the two they had used the day before, along with a fresh pad of paper. Chelsea watched him indulgently as he carefully set out three places on the small, marble-topped table. It was difficult now to believe that he had come so close to death a few short hours ago. Children were so resilient, thank heaven.

She turned her head as Nikos emerged from the room, heart leaping as she took in the muscular power of his thighs revealed by the blue denim shorts. He looked so different out of the formal attire; she had a sudden mind's-eye vision of how he would look out of any attire at all.

"Ready to play?" she asked, hoping her voice didn't betray her thoughts.

"Would I be here if not?" he returned with a derisive glint.

"I will choose the first word," announced Dimitris importantly, already scribing the dashes. "It has six letters. For each one of them you guess right you can draw a line of your hanging man," he told his father. "For each one you guess wrongly I can draw a line of my hanging man. If I finish my drawing before you guess the word, I have won the game. We must play it in English so that Chelsea can play too,'' he added kindly.

''We must teach Chelsea to speak our language,'' Nikos observed, eyes holding hers. ''Then there will be no misunderstanding between us.''

There wasn't anyway, she could have told him. His aim was clear enough in *any* language.

''C,'' she said blandly instead, and received a delighted shake of the head from the younger Pandrossos as he drew in the first line with an enthusiasm that almost snapped the point off the pencil.

''Your turn now,'' he urged his father.

It was Nikos who finally called time on the game, after playing for over an hour. Dimitris would have gone on indefinitely—especially as he was three up. Unlike some children Chelsea could think of, he didn't sulk when told that was enough for the day, settling quite happily to filling a fresh page with matchstick figures.

''It isn't very often that I have the opportunity to indulge myself this way,'' Nikos remarked as he leant back in his seat, hands clasped comfortably behind his head.

''Probably because you don't take advantage of it when it's there,'' Chelsea responded, finding it difficult to keep her eyes from the semi-reclining taut-muscled body. ''It's always the same with you tycoons. Work is all you think about!''

''Not *all*,'' came the soft reply. ''Not even *at* all right now.'' His regard skimmed the length of her body, coming to rest on the face devoid of any hint of make-up with an expression that tensed her insides as if a hand had reached out and squeezed everything together. ''I've never before known a woman who could look even more beautiful without artifice than with it!''

"You should see me first thing in the morning!" she said deprecatingly, and felt warm colour flood her cheeks as his brows lifted in mocking acknowledgement.

"I anticipate doing that."

Chelsea shot a glance at Dimitris. He seemed totally absorbed in what he was doing, but one never knew with children. Not that anything his father had said could be termed unsuitable on the face of it for young ears.

"Do you sail your yacht alone?" she asked, looking for a safer subject.

"It can be handled alone, but there's plenty of space for passengers if you'd like to take a sail yourself," Nikos answered.

"I didn't mean to imply—" she began.

"I didn't suppose that you did," he interjected. "But the notion is a good one. If your ankle allows it, we might take the *Aphrodite* out tomorrow."

"Providing you're not called away again."

"Providing that, yes." He reached out unexpectedly to smooth a stray lock of blonde hair out of her eyes. "It would have to be a dire emergency."

Skin tingling from the touch of those long, lean fingers, Chelsea made a valiant effort to gain control of herself. A push-over wasn't in it!

"Why *Aphrodite?*" she asked, and he smiled.

"Like the goddess of love, she can be fickle and capricious when the mood takes her."

"But you, of course, brook no such nonsense from her!"

The smile deepened. "I find her responsive to my handling."

Chelsea didn't doubt it. She was responding herself right now, and he wasn't even touching her. "I'd love a sail,'' she said hurriedly. ''I'm sure Dimitris would too.''

''Yes!'' agreed the latter eagerly, belying his apparent preoccupation.

''Then I shall be delighted to indulge the both of you,'' his father answered.

There was a pause, a sudden hardening of expression as he glanced at the gold Rolex encircling his wrist. ''For now, however, there are other matters to be dealt with.''

It didn't take a sleuth to guess what they were, Chelsea thought as he rose abruptly from the chair and disappeared indoors. If Ledra hadn't put in an appearance by now, she almost certainly wasn't going to, which meant that whatever steps Nikos had in mind must be put into effect. She wondered if he would call for police help in tracing the woman. Criminal neglect might be one possible charge.

The afternoon drew into early evening, with Dimitris showing no inclination to leave her. He made no mention at all of Ledra. It was as if he had already dismissed her from his mind.

Food was brought at six. Enough for two, if the *despinis* felt in need of sustenance, the young servant, whose name was Costas, pointed out. The master, he said in answer to Chelsea's query, was engaged on the telephone again at present. Possibly a call to cancel whatever arrangement he had made for tonight, thought Chelsea with an edge of cynicism.

At seven, with still no sign of Nikos, she donned the nanny mantle and told Dimitris it was time for bed. He rode to his room on her lap, telling her which way to steer the chair, the two of them giggling together as they ricocheted off doorjambs due to Chelsea's inability to gauge the gap.

Baths could wait, she decided, seeing the boy's energy start to flag as he undressed. He had seemed fine all afternoon, but that wasn't to say that his system was fully recovered from the shock. Sleep was the best remedy.

He had storybooks in English as well as Greek. The tale he chose to have read to him was only a couple of pages long, but he was out of it before she was halfway through. He didn't stir even when she let out a muffled yelp on stubbing her bare toes against the doorjamb on the way out. Tomorrow, come what may, she was back on her own two feet, she vowed. She would have arm muscles like a road-digger if she had to do this for very long!

She was back in her own room, with both doors left ajar so that she would hear if Dimitris cried out, when Nikos finally put in appearance. He had changed his clothing once again, and was now wearing casual white trousers and a dark green shirt.

"I'm sorry to leave you for so long," he apologised. "I glanced in on Dimitris as I passed. He looks very peaceful."

"There don't seem to be any ill-effects," Chelsea agreed. "He's looking forward to going out on the *Aphrodite* tomorrow. Always providing you were serious about it."

"I make no careless promises," he assured her. "But, as I also said, it will depend upon the state of your ankle."

"A yacht being no place for invalids, you mean?"

"I was thinking more in terms of pain."

"It doesn't hurt any more. Look…" She swung the

injured member in a circle, first clockwise then anti-clockwise, ignoring the twinges. "The swelling is just about gone."

"We'll see what the morning brings," came the firm response. "For tonight, you will please me by staying in the chair."

"*All* night?" she asked guilelessly.

His mouth curved. "You will, I think, find the bed more conducive."

He was referring to sleep, of course, she told herself, trying not to read innuendo where it wasn't intended.

"I assume Ledra hasn't turned up?" she said, opting for a change of subject anyway.

The smile faded. "Not as yet."

"You think she might still be on the island?"

"Unless the gardener has a boat of his own unknown to anyone else, there's no way she could have left it."

"So there's no sign of him either?" Chelsea caught herself up, biting her lip. "I'm sorry. It must be the last thing you want to talk about."

"Only in the sense that the subject moves me to an anger I find difficult to control," Nikos acknowledged. "When I think how close Dimitris came to losing his life the same way—" He broke off, jaw tensed. "They can neither of them be allowed to escape justice."

He'd been going to say "the same way his mother lost hers', Chelsea presumed. She wished she dared give way to the urge to get up from the chair and go put her arms about him.

The dark eyes softened as they registered the expression in hers. He came, as before, to take her face between his hands, smoothing her lips with the balls of his thumbs before bending to kiss her lingeringly. Chelsea answered without restraint, longing for him to lift her from the chair and lay her on the bed—*needing* to know him the way she had never known any man before. She could feel his heat, sense his arousal. He wanted her the same way she wanted him. For how long was of no consequence.

The discreet knock on the door he had almost but not quite closed went ignored by both of them. Only when it was repeated more insistently did Nikos reluctantly break off the embrace.

"*Ne?*" he called.

Chelsea didn't understand the reply, but it was enough to alter Nikos's whole attitude.

"They've been found," he said tersely. "I must go."

He was moving as he spoke, the hardness of his jaw boding ill for the two fugitives. Chelsea watched him go in mingled frustration and empathy. There was no doubt where his priorities lay.

CHAPTER EIGHT

COSTAS brought more food at nine, but simply shook his head when asked if Kirios Pandrossos had returned. By eleven-thirty Chelsea could find no further excuse to stay up.

Lying sleepless in bed, she found her imagination running riot with regard to what might have happened to Ledra and Stavros. Not that she thought Nikos capable of murder, but neither did she see him showing the two of them much in the way of clemency. There was every possibility that he wouldn't be prepared to discuss the matter either, which would leave her with a lifelong conjecture.

She dozed off eventually, waking some untold time later when two strong arms slid about her, hauling her close against a broad chest while a pair of wonderfully mobile and passionate lips claimed hers.

Her response was immediate, no thought in her mind of resistance. She felt rather than heard the soft exclamation as she shifted her lower body into closer contact, seeking the hard heat of him with a hunger she couldn't and didn't want to control.

He was naked, skin smooth over rippling muscle, body hair stimulating in its wiry texture. Without conscious volition, she sought the proud manhood, thrilling to the pulsing power. He drew in a long, slow breath as she ran supple, exploratory fingers over him, allowing her instincts to surmount her lack of experience in pleasuring a man.

Nikos removed her short nightdress and tossed it aside, pressing kisses down the length of her throat to seek the twin peaks. The touch of his lips and tongue on her tingling flesh was agony and ecstasy rolled into one. She wanted the sensation to go on for ever, yet at the same time knew that it wasn't enough. What she craved was the merging of her body with his: to be possessed by him in totality.

Her stomach muscles fluttered like a trapped bird's wings as he moved on slowly down the length of her. His hand parted her trembling thighs, sliding between them to find the moist nub and bring her to the very brink before replacing the hand with mouth and tongue, the two combining to drive her right over the edge.

Still in the grip of that tumultuous explosion, Chelsea was aware of him levering himself upright for a moment. Then he was back over her, the breadth of his shoulders shutting out all but a glimmer of moonlight, eyes dark pools in the tautly etched face. The feel of him as he began a slow incursion was exquisite. She spread her legs further to take him, gasping at the burgeoning pressure. Pain seized her for a moment too fleeting to register with any impact, followed by a wonderful sense of completeness as he filled her.

"Yineka," he said softly.

She was lost in sheer sensation when he started to move, her whole being centred on that driving force. When she climaxed it was like nothing she had ever imagined even in her wildest dreams—a breathtaking, body-arching transport. As from a great distance, she heard Nikos groan as he too reached the zenith.

So at last she knew what it was all about, came the fleeting thought, before her mind closed down altogether in the drained aftermath.

It was Nikos who stirred first, lifting himself on his elbows to look down at her with an unreadable expression on his face.

"You do me a great honour," he said. "But why have you waited so long to know a man?"

Chelsea said huskily, "What makes you so sure I never have before?"

"There's a certain resistance which must be broken through the first time. I was aware of it in you." He paused. "Does this mean you're not protected?"

Up until this moment, Chelsea hadn't given that aspect a thought. The possibility of what might have happened through her irresponsibility dried her throat.

"I've never considered it necessary," she admitted. "There hasn't been anyone else I ever wanted to...go this far with." She made a valiant attempt to lighten the atmosphere. "It's a good thing one of us had some foresight!"

"Is it not?" he agreed drily. There was another pause, a change of tone. "That apart, you have no regrets?"

Regrets! Chelsea touched the tip of her tongue to lips still swollen from his kisses, feeling the deep-down, wholly pleasurable ache. How could *anyone* regret such an experience? She'd been taken to the heights; whatever the depths to come, it was worth it.

"Not a one!" she said, with a certainty that drew a smile to the firm mouth. "It was...incredible!"

Nikos gave a low laugh. "For me too. There are few women selfless enough to think of giving pleasure before they themselves have been satiated—if they think of it at all. You almost robbed me of control in the beginning."

"As if a mere female could do that!" she bantered, and saw a spark light the darkness.

"No *mere* female could. You're a very special kind."

If by no means the only kind, came the thought, discarded with purpose. "At the risk of sounding downright greedy," she said softly, "do you think we could do it again?"

"As many times as I can manage," he assured her, eliciting a wide-eyed wonder.

"You mean there's a limit?"

"One you might reach very soon if you don't start showing me a proper respect!" he retaliated.

"I do respect you." She could say that with truth. What she couldn't acknowledge was the deeper emotion, because it wasn't what he wanted from her.

She slid her hands along the broad shoulders, tremoring to the feel of rippling muscle. Desire rose in her again like mercury in a heatwave. "I want you!" she whispered, shutting out everything but that one fact. "Want you, want you, want—"

He stopped her mouth with his, passion flaring swift and fierce to match her own. In this way she could want nothing more was her last rational thought.

The pillow at her side was empty when she opened her eyes on daylight, although the feel of his arms still lingered.

Chelsea went hot at the memory of last night's abandonment, hardly able to believe that she could have acted with such a total lack of inhibition. There was no part of her that Nikos didn't know intimately—no part of *him* that *she* didn't know with equal intimacy. Only in the physical sense, though. His mind was a closed book still.

It was possible, she reflected wryly, that his appetite for her might have been surfeited after such excesses.

According to the pundits, women were supposed to retain a certain element of mystery to keep a man's interest. Too late now, anyway. She had given her all.

At least her ankle appeared to have suffered no ill-effects, she discovered, trying it out tentatively while sitting on the edge of the bed. Providing she took a degree of care, she could probably discard the wheelchair.

Her cotton wrap was draped over a chair a few feet away. Only when she got up to reach for it did she notice the faint bruises on her upper arms where Nikos's fingers had grasped her. So far as she could recall, she only had one T-shirt with enough sleeve to cover the marks, and they were going to last considerably longer than the one day. If Dimitris noted them, he was going to be asking some awkward questions.

There were times when it was necessary to bend the truth a little, she acknowledged. Not that she imagined the staff would be deceived as to their origin. There was even a possibility that they'd one and all find their employer's canniness in securing a nanny—albeit a temporary one—for his son along with a pillow-friend for himself wholly admirable.

Stop carping, she told herself determinedly at that point. She'd been under no compulsion to accept the arrangement. If it did turn out that Nikos had exhausted his personal interest in her, then she would have to live with it. What she *wasn't* going to do was abandon Dimitris.

She made it to the bathroom on foot with little difficulty, emerging ten minutes later fully dressed in one of her multi-hued skirts and a white cotton blouse. With sandals offering little support for an ankle still retaining a certain weakness, she was forced to settle once more for the trainers that had been fetched up from the beach,

incongruous though they looked with the rest of her out-
fit. At least if they did go out on the yacht she could
change into shorts.

It was still only a little after seven o'clock. Chelsea
took a cautious look into Dimitris's room, to find him
still fast asleep, curled up like a puppy on a bed devoid
of covers. Smiling, she went to pick them up from the
floor and cover the small body. He stirred, and murmured something, but he didn't waken.

Returning to her own room, she went out onto the
balcony to stand looking out at the great blue bowl of
sea and sky. The air was clean and fresh, untainted by
city pollution. Chelsea drew in deep breaths of it, filling
her lungs to capacity. Life here had to be a great deal
healthier than where she came from.

Not so in Athens, of course. The city was reputed to
be one of the worst in the world when it came to air
quality. It was to the good that Nikos wasn't domiciled
there on a permanent basis.

Switching her attention down to the courtyard, she felt
muscle and sinew contract on sight of the subject of her
thoughts, talking with an older man whose garb of dark
trousers and white shirt certified his position. Nikos was
dressed in the same denim shorts he had worn yesterday—or another pair like them—with a white T-shirt
that fitted his frame like a second skin. He had one foot
raised to rest easily on the edge of a stone flower tub,
weight supported on the elbow resting along his bent
knee. The sun struck a healthy glint in the thickly curling
pelt of dark hair.

As if sensing her gaze, he looked up, a smile lighting
his face as he lifted a hand in greeting. Chelsea waved
back, heedless now of what the man at his side might
be thinking in her relief at the realisation that her fears

had been groundless. It was obvious that Nikos didn't care if the staff knew what they had become to each other, so why should she?

A sound behind her drew her eyes quickly round to where Dimitris stood in the doorway, rubbing his eyes.

"I dreamed you had gone away," he said plaintively. "You will never go away, will you?"

Chelsea bit her lip, wondering how to explain the temporary nature of her position here to the child without upsetting him. He had taken to her with a thoroughness she hadn't anticipated. Gratifying though the attachment was, it posed a real dilemma.

"I'll be here while I'm needed," she said in the end, forced to settle for prevarication. She lightened her voice to add, "It's a lovely day for our sail!"

He brightened immediately, relieving her of the fear that he might not want to go near water at all after what he'd been through. "Your ankle is good again?"

"Yes. Look…" She took a few steps, trying not to put any weight on the weaker joint. "Good as new!"

"When are we to go?" he asked, more than ready to be convinced.

"As soon as we've eaten, I'd think." Chelsea hoped she wasn't being over-optimistic. "Which means you'd better go and get dressed. After you have a bath," she tagged on as he started to turn, stopping him in his tracks.

"I'm not in need of a bath!" he declared, in the indignant tones employed by small boys all over the world. "How could I become dirty when I'm asleep in bed?"

"You missed having one last night," Chelsea pointed out, hiding a smile at his choice of word.

"I was clean last night too!"

Easy to see whose son he was, she thought drily. Nobody put one over on a Pandrossos. "Well, at least you can give your face and hands a lick and a promise," she compromised, reluctant to make an issue of it.

Dimitris gave a gurgle of laughter. "My tongue won't reach far enough!"

Chelsea grinned back. "So you'll just have to use a sponge instead. You've got ten minutes!"

Eyes sparkling, he vanished in the direction he had come, leaving her to wonder just what she had let herself in for. Between father and son, she wasn't going to know whether she was standing on her head or her heels!

Not even five minutes had passed when he returned, already dressed in clean shorts and T-shirt. Judging from the damp curls of hair at the front, he had carried out the instruction to the letter. He looked so angelic, Chelsea couldn't resist sweeping him up in a bear hug, losing her footing in the process and falling backwards onto the bed to the tune of his delighted screams.

"Again!" he demanded. "Do it again!"

She tickled him instead, provoking an immediate retaliation. Breathless with laughter, she sought to hold him off so that she could get up, but it was like wrestling with an eel.

"Is it possible that the two of you might find time for breakfast?" asked Nikos. "Or should I leave you to your play?"

"Yes!" shouted his son, not in the least thrown to find him in the room.

"No!" declared Chelsea hastily. She managed to thrust the child aside long enough to sit up, conscious of her dishevelled hair and clothing, and of the amusement in Nikos's eyes as he surveyed her. "We were just coming down," she claimed.

"So I see." He shook his head as Dimitris curled his fingers in readiness for another attack. "Enough. You'll wear Chelsea out."

If he didn't do it first, she thought. Looking at him now, so big and dark and devastating, she yearned to be with him again the way she had been in the night. He was everything a man should be, and so rarely was. Falling in love with him had been inevitable. What she had to face was the impermanence of the affair. Still no regrets, though. If nothing else, she would have these few weeks to look back on.

"Just give me a minute to tidy myself up," she said, getting to her feet and smoothing her skirt down. "I'll be right behind you."

"I've no objection to waiting," Nikos returned equably. "All you need is a brush through your hair. The rest of you is perfectly presentable."

And I should know, said the glint in his eyes, bringing a sudden warmth to her cheeks.

Chelsea found a kind of intimacy in brushing her hair back into order while he watched. She could see him through the mirror, lounging easily against the doorjamb, a thumb hooked into the belt of his shorts. For a brief moment she could imagine what it might be like to be married to him.

Fat chance of *that* happening! she thought wryly.

After seeing her walk across the room, Nikos appeared to accept that her ankle was proving no great problem this morning, and Chelsea certainly had no intention of risking a cancellation of the promised expedition by admitting to any weakness. She accompanied father and son down the stairs without faltering.

Continental-style breakfast was served outside on the upper terrace. Chelsea was halfway down her second cup

of the excellent coffee when Costas came out to tell
Nikos he was wanted on the telephone. Catching
Dimitris's suddenly downcast expression as his father
went to answer the call, she felt her own heart sink in
like assumption. A call at this hour could only mean
trouble of one kind or another.

It was obvious when Nikos returned that their fears
were confirmed.

"I'm afraid the problems have not yet been resolved," he announced. "I must return."

"I want to sail on the sea!" wailed Dimitris, unable
this time to accept the disappointment without complaint.

"Enough!" his father reprimanded. "There'll be other
times to go sailing. I'm sorry," he added for Chelsea's
benefit. "It's essential that I show myself."

"Have you any idea how long you might be gone?"
she asked, trying to sound calm and collected about it
when inside she wanted to follow Dimitris's example
and wail her disappointment.

He lifted his shoulders. "Perhaps a day, perhaps more.
Who can tell?" The eyes meeting hers gave the impression of a mind already immersed in more important matters. "The helicopter will be here in minutes. I must go
and change my clothing."

Chelsea gave Dimitris a sympathetic smile as his father left them, receiving a distinctly wobbly one in return.

"Never mind," she said, "it will be something to
look forward to in a day or two."

From the look on the small face, that was no comfort.
Chelsea couldn't blame him. To a five-year-old, a day
or two might just as well be a year or two.

"It's not your papa's fault," she said gently. "It's his

job. I'm sure he'll be back as soon as he possibly can."
She briskened her voice. "Anyway, we can amuse ourselves in the meantime. How about hide and seek, for
instance?" She plumped for a game she was pretty sure
would be universally known. "There must be lots of
places to hide here."

He brightened a little. "I can hide first?"

"Yes. But we must wait to wave goodbye to your
father before we start." She pricked up her ears as the
familiar sound impinged on her consciousness. "Here
comes the helicopter now! Let's go and watch it land."

Dimitris scrambled to join her as she got up from the
table, not at all loath to take the hand she held out invitingly and walk with her to the archway. The machine
was approaching fast, the yellow and white fuselage
bright in the sunlight. From where they stood, it was
possible to see down to the level containing the landing
pad. Chelsea let go of the boy's hand in order to slide a
casual arm about his shoulders as the helicopter came in
to hover like some huge bird of prey before sinking to
the ground, well able to understand why Nikos preferred
to keep the great noisy things for emergency transportation only.

Dressed now in another superbly cut suit, this time in
dark blue, he came into view, striding purposefully from
the house. He carried no overnight case, Chelsea noted.
In all probability he kept a full wardrobe of clothes
wherever it was he stayed when he was in Athens.

"All set?" she asked brightly as he reached the two
of them, mentally cursing the stupidity of the question.
"We thought we'd wave you off from here," she added.

"And then we're going to play hide and seek," im-
parted Dimitris, with an air of "see what you'll be missing!".

Nikos kept a grave face, apart from a faint twitch at the corners of his mouth. "I'll think of you enjoying yourselves while I toil."

He bent and swept the child up in a embrace that warmed Chelsea's heart, planting a kiss on top of the curly head.

"Do as Chelsea tells you," he instructed. "She is in charge of everything and everyone while I'm away."

"That's an awful lot of responsibility!" she protested as he set the child down again. "Surely—"

"You'll cope with it," Nikos responded firmly. "You're capable of coping with anything life may throw at you. You already proved that much to me."

He had more faith in her than she had in herself, Chelsea could have told him. On the other hand, it was unlikely that anything else untoward would happen over the next day or two. Lightning didn't strike twice in the same place.

She was destitute, though unsurprised, when he failed to kiss her goodbye. He was hardly going to show intimacy of that nature in front of his son. The two of them watched him descend to the waiting helicopter in shared deprivation—the forerunner, Chelsea imagined, of many such occasions to come during the next few weeks. If nothing else, she could make sure Dimitris was looked after the way he should be when his father wasn't here to do it.

They were still hiding and seeking at eleven, when Costas brought out refreshments, with Dimitris claiming a forfeit after Chelsea had failed to find him squeezed into a storage locker under the courtyard steps.

"I'll think very hard about what you are to do," he said.

"Just keep it within the realms of possibility," Chelsea urged. "Remember I'm still an invalid."

"You told Papa your ankle was mended," he reminded her. "Were you not saying the truth?"

Caught on the hop, she floundered for a moment, giving way to wry laughter as she caught the mischievous sparkle in the dark eyes. "It's called tactical prevarication," she admitted. "That means—"

"It means that you told Papa what you wanted him to think was the truth."

Chelsea gave up. There was just no beating a Pandrossos down, whatever age. "I wanted to go on the *Aphrodite*," she admitted. "As it turned out, I needn't have bothered. It just goes to show…"

Dimitris was no longer listening, she saw. His gaze had gone beyond her, face lighting up. "Dion!"

Chelsea turned slowly to look at the man who had just emerged from the house, preparing herself for the reprobation she was pretty sure would be coming her way. The expression on Dion's face was certainly far from friendly.

"If you think Nikos can be persuaded to grant you your wish because of what you did yesterday, you're wrong!" he declared, ignoring his young cousin's presence. "He may even consider that you arranged your own accident in order to stay here at all!"

There was a very good chance of it, Chelsea conceded. Given the truth, as Dion knew it, he was certainly unlikely to believe that her professional interests were no longer of any note.

"Dion and I have to speak together in private," she said to Dimitris, who was obviously puzzled by his cousin's harangue. "Would you give us a few minutes, please?"

Her smile apparently offered reassurance that nothing was wrong. "I'll go and fetch my pinball game," he said. "Dion hasn't yet seen it."

Chelsea waited until he was halfway up the steps, and out of earshot, before turning back to face whatever was coming to her.

"Are you going to tell Nikos what you know?" she asked bluntly, seeing no point in beating about the bush.

"You deserve no less," Dion retorted, "for the pain you've inflicted on my sister!"

"I've done nothing to Florina," Chelsea protested. "She and your mother have been living a dream where Nikos is concerned."

Dion scowled. "How would you know that?"

"Because he told me so himself." Chelsea made a gesture of appeal. "She's wasting her life, Dion. It's time someone made her realise it—made you *all* realise it!"

A variety of expressions chased across the handsome features, settling finally into sullen acceptance. "Nikos knew what was expected. He should have made his intentions clear before this."

"Perhaps he hoped the hint would be taken."

"Perhaps *you* hope to take up the position for yourself," Dion snapped back.

Her laugh sounded more than a little brittle. "Let's not get ridiculous! I'm here only because I injured my ankle."

"You're here because Nikos wants you in his bed," came the cutting reply. "If he hasn't already had you there." He caught the fleeting expression in her eyes, and gave a sneering smile. "But of course he has!"

It was a waste of time and effort denying it, Chelsea

concluded. Why should she, anyway? She wasn't ashamed of what she'd done.

She lifted her shoulders, searching the dark eyes for some sign of the man she had first known. "Dion, can't you just forget about the interview idea? As I already said, it was a bad one to start with. I'm sorry about Florina, really I am, but it has nothing whatsoever to do with me. Believe me."

For a moment it was touch and go, then his expression moderated just a little. "You give me your word that nothing you learn about the Pandrossoses will ever be printed?"

"Without reservation," she assured him.

"Then I may keep your secret."

May, she noted, not will. She briefly contemplated insisting on a promise, but didn't want to risk putting his back up any further than it already was. In any case, it was the action—or lack of it—that counted in the end, not the word.

"Thanks," she said, doing her best to sound properly grateful. "Would you like some coffee? Costas just brought out a fresh pot. Or I can order you something else."

Dion curled a lip. "If I wanted something else I would order it for myself."

Chelsea made no answer on the grounds that whatever she said it was going to be taken the wrong way. The sight of Costas bringing out another cup and saucer was a relief. She gave the young man a warm smile as she thanked him, happy to have it returned. It was odds on that the whole of the staff were fully aware by now of the situation between her and their employer, but if Costas was anything to go by there was no censure extended in her direction. That in itself gave her a much needed boost.

CHAPTER NINE

DION took a seat under the shade of an umbrella, eyes still devoid of their former light-hearted sparkle.

"How long will you be staying here?" he asked abruptly.

"Until Nikos finds a reliable nurse," Chelsea returned.

His expression underwent a subtle alteration. "He's employing you to take care of Dimitris?"

"No, I'm doing it for free." She kept her tone level with an effort. "It's hardly an onerous task. As you yourself told me, he's a real little character."

"And by becoming close to him you hope to become even closer to his father." It was a statement, not a question. "Nikos would never consider marrying a non-Greek, whatever tricks you use!"

Chelsea clamped down hard on any leaning towards despondency. "It hadn't occurred to me that he might. I'm staying for Dimitris's sake, not my own."

It was obvious that Dion didn't believe a word of it. She doubted if anything she could say would convince him. She couldn't blame him for feeling the way he did. He'd brought her to Skalos to help *his* cause, not to provide his cousin with a bedmate.

"Have you seen anything of Elini since the party?" she asked, hoping to abandon the subject.

"Why would it concern you whether I had or had not?" he returned peevishly.

"Because we were friends, and friendship is about caring."

"You care nothing for me," he declared. "Only for yourself. The moment you saw Nikos, I was nothing to you!"

"That's not true." Chelsea refused to allow the irritation she was beginning to feel to surface. "I didn't plan for any of this to happen. It just…did. And for the record," she added, "I know exactly where I stand."

He was silent a moment, studying her, the struggle going on inside him more than apparent.

"Nikos is fortunate," he said at length. "As the one who saved the life of his son, you're in a position to ask a great deal more of him than a temporary place in his life."

"Perhaps a temporary place is all I'm interested in," she rejoined, attempting to sound matter-of-fact about it. "I have a life of my own waiting for me back home."

Recrimination gave way to something approaching admiration. "I know no other girl who thinks the way you do! Have you no desire to marry at all?"

"Never say never," she quipped. "Who knows what the fates have in store? *You* may even finish up marrying Elini. If it's what you'd like to do, that is."

"Yes." Both tone and expression had softened. "She's the only one I've ever wanted to take to wife."

"Then for heaven's sake let her know it," Chelsea urged, forsaking her vow not to become involved again. "I think you might find her receptive enough."

Dion's whole face underwent a transformation. "You think?"

"All right, so I know you will." Chelsea was past trying to keep the ball in the air. "You weren't the only one attempting to arouse a little jealousy the other day."

"Elini told you this?"

"Yes. I advised her to keep on playing it cool for a while, but if you really do feel the way you say you do about her, why hang about? You know where she is, so go get her!"

"I will!" Fired with new life, all else forgotten, Dion got to his feet. "This moment!"

He offered no word of thanks. Not that Chelsea was expecting it anyway. Remembering what Nikos had said about the probable impermanency of Dion's feelings for the girl, she knew a momentary doubt, but it was too late now to undo what she had done. All she could do was hope for the best.

Dimitris was on his way back with the precious pinball machine in his hand. Dion gave him a pat on the head in passing, but was too intent on his own pursuits to pay heed to his young cousin's disappointment. Her fault, thought Chelsea ruefully, viewing the crestfallen little face. It had all better be worth it!

Nikos returned in the late afternoon of the third day after his departure. There had been no message from him between times, so the first Chelsea knew of it was when the helicopter put in an appearance. Even then she couldn't be sure it wasn't Dr Kalvos paying an unscheduled visit.

She and Dimitris went to the top of the steps to await the arrival, the latter jumping with joy when he saw his father mounting towards them. Chelsea managed to maintain an outer decorum while her stomach tied itself in knots of anticipation as her eyes devoured the forceful features. She had missed him so much—and not just in the purely physical sense.

"Everything sorted?" she asked lightly when Dimitris's first flush of enthusiasm had abated.

"For now," Nikos confirmed. "I may be required to settle other points of dispute."

"But you won't be going away again tomorrow?" queried Dimitris anxiously, and received a reassuring smile.

"Tomorrow we sail in the *Aphrodite.*' Dark eyes sought vivid blue, the expression in them causing Chelsea's heart to perform a record-beating high jump. "So tonight we must all of us retire to our beds early in order to be fully charged with energy for the day."

"I am *always* in my bed early," declared his son, on a note that suggested it might be a little *too* early for his tastes. "Will you and Chelsea be going to bed when I do?"

"Perhaps a little later," Nikos replied, with an equanimity belied by the amusement lurking at the corners of his mouth. "Adults don't need quite as much sleep as children."

Dimitris digested that in silence for a moment. "When *I* am old," he said at length, "I shall stay up *all* night!"

They had reached the house. Laughing openly now, Nikos swept the boy up and tossed him over a shoulder, running up the steps with Dimitris screaming delightedly. Chelsea followed, feeling a little left out. Ridiculous, of course. Did she expect Nikos to toss *her* over the other shoulder? The two of them were family; she was merely a hanger-on.

They were barely indoors when Costas appeared with the dreaded word *"telephono"* on his lips. Not already! thought Chelsea despairingly as Nikos swung his son to the floor in order to take the call on the hall extension.

"Ne?" he said shortly.

Watching his face, as was Dimitris at her side, Chelsea saw his expression alter. When he spoke again it was on a softer note, the words themselves incomprehensible to her, unlike the smile curving the firm lips.

It was almost certainly a woman on the other end of the line—and not an employee either. Someone, she conjectured, in a position to make an accurate assessment of how long it would have taken him to get here; someone he'd left yearning just to hear his voice again. She knew that feeling herself.

She drew Dimitris away, reluctant to be caught listening to what he was saying whether she could understand it or not. He'd been away three nights. Why would she imagine he would have spent any one of them alone? There was every possibility that he kept a permanent mistress in Athens for such times.

There was little to be gleaned from his expression when he came to where they sat reading together in the *saloni*. Dimitris eyed him anxiously.

"Are you to go away again?"

The shake of the dark head was enough to bring a smile back to the child's face. Chelsea couldn't bring herself to fully meet the gaze turned her way.

"I have things I must do," he said. "You will join me for a drink before we eat?"

"Of course." She could hardly have said no, even if she had wanted to. "See you then."

His brows had drawn together a little, but he made no comment, just nodded and departed. Even if he connected her withdrawal to the telephone call, Chelsea doubted if he would appreciate her feelings. He'd made no commitment to her. So far as he was concerned, they were simply two people who happened to share a mutual desire.

One he had every intention of satisfying again tonight, from the way he had looked at her on arrival. What she had to consider was whether she could accept the likelihood of his having been with another woman this very afternoon—precautions taken or not.

He was already waiting in the *saloni* when she went down at eight-thirty. Wearing a black shirt tonight, hips lean in a pair of the pale cream trousers he seemed to favour for evenings, he looked dynamic. Chelsea felt her heartstrings start strumming as he ran a glance over her slender length in the red shift dress.

"I'm afraid my wardrobe is very limited," she said. "You've seen just about the whole of it now."

"A beautiful woman has no need of adornment," he returned. "What would you like?"

You, she thought hungrily, acknowledging the impossibility of what she had been contemplating. Even if there were other women in his life, she couldn't give him up. Not yet at any rate.

"Gin and tonic, please," she said, hoping her voice didn't betray her.

"Ice and lemon?"

"Lovely." She moved to take a seat on the same sofa where Nikos had set her down the evening she had hurt her ankle—not even a week ago yet. If she hadn't taken that fall, she would have been long gone now. When she thought about what she would have missed...

"I spoke to my uncle a short time ago," said Nikos, handing her a glass. "He tells me that Dion made a formal declaration of his wish to marry Elini Verikiou." The pause was weighted. "I'm also told that Dion was here the day I went to Athens. Was it you who persuaded him to do as he did?"

He hadn't taken a seat himself. Chelsea looked up to

study the carved features, not all that certain of his mood any more.

"'Persuaded'—no," she said.

"But the subject was discussed?"

"Well…yes."

"And you advised him that his addresses would be welcomed?"

"I told him what Elini told me," she admitted. "I didn't really expect him to go straight round and propose, but if they both feel the same way it's surely not such a bad thing?"

"Except that Dion is in no position to acquire a wife. He has no income, other than what his mother provides."

"Couldn't he be found something within the company?" Chelsea ventured.

Nikos gave a thin smile. "The company, as you would say, carries no passengers. Dion has never shown any interest in work of any kind. He prefers to play."

"But he'll know he can't carry on that way now he has marriage in mind, so surely—"

"Dion's isn't the only wish to be taken into account. Thannasis Verikiou has a more reliable prospect in mind."

Chelsea made a small sound of protest. "Doesn't what Elini wants count either?"

"Elini allows her emotions to overrule her. A good marriage is based on far more important considerations."

"Love surely plays *some* part?"

"Not necessarily."

Chelsea kept her gaze fixed on the glass she held in her fingers. "If there's no bond of that nature at all, there can't be very much joy in marital relations."

"You consider love essential to the enjoyment of sexual intercourse?"

Her heart jerked. "In marriage, yes," she said hurriedly. "Otherwise it surely just becomes a duty to be performed in order to procreate."

"So you could never yourself marry a man you didn't love?"

Blue eyes lifted as if drawn by an invisible force to view the enigmatic expression. If only, she thought achingly, she could just this once tell what he was really thinking and feeling. If only she dared let go and say what *she* really felt, regardless!

"No, I couldn't," she said instead.

"Even if you had to go through life alone because you never found a man you could love to such an extent?"

"Even then." The pause was brief, the urge overpowering. "You said once that if *you* married again it would be to someone of your own choice—which suggests that you were forced into much the same thing you're saying Elini should accept."

"That's a different matter."

"No, it isn't." Chelsea wasn't prepared to back down. "If you really believed love was the least consideration, you'd have married Florina. She has to be eminently suitable in every other respect."

His own drink still untouched, Nikos considered her dispassionately. "You doubt that I loved Dimitris's mother?"

"Did you?" she challenged.

For a moment it seemed doubtful that he was going to answer the question at all, then he lifted his shoulders in a brief shrug.

"Regretfully, no. She was very beautiful, but beauty is only a part of what draws a man to a woman."

"Do you think she loved you?"

"The matter was never discussed. Whether or not, she was all that a wife should be."

Chelsea said softly, "And she gave you Dimitris."

"Yes." The dark eyes took on a warmer glow. "For that I will always be grateful—as I will so to you, for saving his life." He briskened his voice. "Enough of this introspection. Enough of Dion too!"

It was pushing it, but Chelsea felt she had to at least make the attempt. "Elini's father might listen to you if you put in a word on his behalf."

Nikos looked unmoved. "Even if I wished to intervene, I have no authority over the Verikious' private and personal affairs." He shook his head as she opened her mouth again. "There's nothing more to be said on the subject."

Blue eyes sparked. "Is that an order?"

"A statement." There was an answering spark in the black depths. "Dion must make his own plea."

A pretty hopeless one, Chelsea reckoned, quelling the defiant surge in the sure knowledge that she would be wasting time and breath on any further exhortation. When it came to choosing wisely, she and Dion made a fine pair!

Nikos put down his glass and took hers from her to do the same, drawing her to her feet. Humour curved his lips as he studied her tensed face.

"You find it difficult still to submit your will to mine?"

"It's nothing to do with wills," she denied. "Or the fact that you're male and I'm female. I'm only a visitor to your country. I can hardly argue with your customs—even if I do consider them archaic.''

Nikos inclined his head. ''Your opinion is duly noted.''

''Don't patronise me!'' she burst out, unable this time to keep a hold on herself. ''I'm no secondary citizen!''

''As you yourself pointed out a moment ago, you're not a citizen here of any kind,'' came the smooth return. ''The reason I allow you so much latitude.''

''You *allow!* Of all the—'' She broke off, seeing the glimmer of laughter in his eyes and dissolving into it herself. ''You did that deliberately,'' she accused.

''Of course. You're magnificent when you're spitting fire and brimstone!''

He put his lips to hers with a touch so light she could scarcely feel it, hands sliding up her arms to her shoulders, holding her still. Not that she had any inclination to move away from that teasing, taunting probe. She would have melted against him, but he wouldn't let her, maintaining a frustrating six inches of distance between them.

It was Nikos who had begun it, and it was Nikos who ended it, putting her from him with a purpose she recognised only too well.

''We save the rest for later,'' he said. ''There's dinner to be eaten first.''

Food was the least of Chelsea's needs right now. She had an idea that it might be his too, but if he wanted to prove himself capable of waiting then so could she.

There was no shortage of conversation throughout the meal. Chelsea had to keep talking in order to stop herself from thinking about what was to come. She asked him about his working life, fascinated by the glimpses he gave her into the running of a company the size of Pandrossos.

"There's so little known about you back home," she remarked incautiously at one point. "On a personal level, I mean."

"The way I intend to keep it," he said. "My private life is my own affair. Any journalist who attempted to violate that privacy would live to regret it."

He spoke calmly enough, but there was no doubting his seriousness. Chelsea felt a tremor run through her. If he discovered who and what she really was, what hope would there be of convincing him that her original aim had long been consigned to never-never land?

Unlikely, she reassured herself. The only person who knew the truth was Dion, and he had no reason to give her away. She would be gone in a few weeks anyway, and then it wouldn't matter.

They returned to the *saloni* for an after-dinner brandy and further inconsequential chat. By ten-thirty, with Nikos showing no indication of retiring, Chelsea could stand the strain no longer.

"I think I'll go to bed," she said, on as casual a note as she could manage.

"If you're tired," he returned without particular inflexion, "then perhaps you should."

"I'm not tired," she denied swiftly—too swiftly. She added hastily, "We were all supposed to be having an early night in order to be fresh for the morning."

"I take it, then, that you prefer not to have my company tonight?"

"No... I mean, that isn't what..." She stopped, eyeing him in sudden fury as he lounged there on the sofa opposite with that half-smile forming on his lips. "You louse!" she exclaimed.

Dark brows drew together; the smile vanished. "What did you call me?"

Chelsea looked at him uncertainly, unable to tell whether he was serious or not. "What's in a name?" she said, trying to make a joke of it.

"If I'm to be likened to a creature that crawls in dirt, a great deal." He was sitting up straighter now, face set in lines that sent a quiver down her spine. "You will apologise!"

Or else what? she wondered, and decided she might be better off not finding out.

"Of course I apologise," she said. "It wasn't meant to insult you."

One dark brow lifted. "The men in your country find the term endearing?"

"Not...exactly."

"But they would put up no objection to having it applied?"

"No. Well, not in the same way, at any rate." Chelsea made a helpless gesture. "Look, it was just one of those things you say without thinking first."

"*I* say nothing without thinking first."

"I didn't mean you, yourself, I meant—" She broke off once more, looking at him suspiciously. "You're having me on again, aren't you?"

The sudden grin gave an almost boyish appeal to the strong features. "If by that you mean I am teasing you, perhaps just a little. The English language is open to misinterpretation. Not that I'm prepared to accept the calling of names on a regular basis, you understand?"

"Of course, Nikos," she said with mock humility.

Humour gave way to something infinitely more stirring as he gazed at her, taking in every detail of her face beneath the golden tumble of her hair, sliding down over the supple curves of her body to dwell on the shapely length of leg revealed by the short red tunic.

"Come here to me," he said softly.

Command or invitation? She was beyond caring. She crossed the few feet between them to slide down into his arms, loving the feel of him, the power of him—loving the man within. She wanted so badly to say the words, but it wouldn't be what he wanted to hear from her.

"I want you," she whispered instead against his lips. "How much longer do I have to wait?"

"Such immodesty from one so recently a virgin," he chided on a light note.

"Your fault for showing me what was missing from my life," she rejoined.

"Then we'd best extend the experience."

Sliding an arm beneath her knees, he rose without effort from the sofa and headed for the door, bearing her weight as if it were nothing. Chelsea cradled her head against the broad shoulder, the limitations forgotten.

Ecstatic as that first night had been, this one surpassed it. Lying wrapped in Nikos's arms, watching his face in the moonlight as he slept, Chelsea hoped it would be a long time before a suitable replacement for Ledra was found.

Once again, she wondered what had happened to the woman and her lover. That Nikos had the power to have the pair of them imprisoned she didn't doubt. If that was the only penalty imposed, they would be lucky. He had looked ready to inflict dire retribution when he'd left her that evening.

He stirred in his sleep, murmuring something she couldn't quite catch. It would have been all Greek to her anyway, she supposed. He was hardly likely to dream in English.

She made a tentative movement to ease her position, only to feel his arms tighten about her. The dark eyes opened, coming to immediate life as they looked into hers. She had believed herself sapped of desire, but she wasn't. Nikos saw to that. Nikos, came the hazy thought as they slid together once more, would always see to it.

CHAPTER TEN

SAILING was everything anticipated. The climate helped, of course, Chelsea had to acknowledge. Given grey skies and a North Sea gale, she might not be quite so enthusiastic.

"There's a different kind of pleasure to be found in running before a storm," Nikos rejoined when she said as much to him. "Challenge is essential to life if it's to be lived to the full."

She could hardly claim to have been all that much of one, Chelsea reflected wryly. Last week at this time they hadn't even met.

Secured to a running safety line, Dimitris was up in the bows, where he could watch the dolphins leaping ahead of the speeding craft. She turned her gaze from him back to the man at the wheel, viewing the strong lines of his body in the white shorts and T-shirt with the customary thrill.

"I'd have thought you could get all the challenge you needed in business," she observed.

"Of a kind, perhaps. But business affairs are only a part of life, not the whole."

"Some people don't *have* a life outside of their work."

Nikos gave her a thoughtful glance. "You speak of someone you know personally?"

She thought of denying it, but there was no real reason to. It had long been established fact.

"My father," she admitted.

"What is his line of business?"

"He's a civil engineer. More often than not he's out of the country. As a child, I scarcely saw him."

"A pity," he agreed, "but that, unfortunately, is the nature of such a calling. Those left at home wanted for nothing, I take it?"

"Materially, no."

"And he spent whatever time he could with his family?"

Chelsea hesitated. "I suppose so, but—"

"Then you were more fortunate than many. Better a father who cared enough to come home when possible than none at all."

The reproof was more sensed than stressed, but it reckoned just the same. "You make me feel a real self-centred bitch!" she said ruefully.

Lips quirking, he ran a glance over her as she lay there in the skimpy bikini, hair spread like spilled gold about her head. "You do yourself an injustice. Anyone who less resembles the mother of a dog I've yet to find!"

"You know what I mean." Chelsea couldn't summon a smile. "I just never looked at it from that angle before."

"So the next time you see your father it may be with fresh eyes."

The next time she saw her father her time here would be over, came the thought, bringing instant depression. She fought it back purposefully. As Nikos himself had said, better a little than nothing at all.

Dimitris came scrambling back to them, chattering away in Greek in his excitement. It was a constant source of amazement to Chelsea that he could switch so easily from one language to the other. Her own grasp of Greek had improved over the past days, but was still in its infancy. Dimitris found her errors in the use of it hilarious.

Nikos allowed him to help steer, standing the child in front of him so that he could grasp the wheel too. Chelsea watched them with a certain envy. If Nikos hadn't loved his wife, he certainly adored his son. The colouring apart, there was little resemblance between the two of them. Like Dion, Dimitris obviously inherited his looks from his mother: more an Apollo than a Hercules. One thing was certain—he was going to be a real heart-stopper in time to come.

It was a day to remember all the way through. Nikos had brought along an ice-box packed to the brim with food and drink. He anchored off-shore of a tiny island inhabited only by birds, and rowed the three of them in the dinghy to a curve of white beach inaccessible from the land.

To anyone seeing them seated there picnicking on the sand they might even appear to be a regular family, thought Chelsea, wishing it could only be true. She loved both father and son. Losing them both when her time was up was going to be unbearable.

She made an effort to cast all such thoughts aside. Live each day as it came, that was the best policy.

Fascinated by the contents of a shallow rock pool, Dimitris expressed a desire to stay a little longer when Nikos suggested it was time to move on to pastures new. Chelsea was in no way loath to disagree with the child. The place was heaven, the company likewise—what more could there be?

"I've eaten too much," she declared, stretching out on the rug Nikos had thoughtfully brought along too. "I'll just lie here till my waistline goes back to normal!"

Nikos leaned over to lay a hand across her bare midriff, smiling as he felt the involuntary contraction beneath his fingers. "Your waistline is as it always was, slender as a wand," he said. "No single line of your body is anything but delicious to the eye." His voice was low, sensual, setting her alight the way it always did. "Were we alone, I would view it in its entirety."

"You can hardly call a bikini much of a cover," Chelsea murmured, and saw the wicked gleam in his eyes spring to life.

"It hides from me the parts of you that I cherish the most. The beautiful breasts my lips long to kiss—that secret place into which no other man has ever penetrated." His voice softened even further, the words a mere whisper, yet every syllable clear. "I know the feel of you, the scent of you, the taste of you, *agapi mou.* You are—"

"Stop it, *please!*" Chelsea couldn't control the shuddering response. "You're not playing fair!"

"To either of us," he agreed. "But then isn't it said that frustration is good for the soul?"

"I don't know about it being good for the soul," she rejoined wryly, "but it wreaks havoc on the system. I feel as if I just went three rounds with Rocky Marciano!"

Nikos gave a shout of laughter and collapsed back onto the rug at her side. "Never," he declared, "have I known a woman like you!"

"I'm English," she said, on as light a note as she could manage. "I'm not used to that kind of rhetoric."

He turned his head to study her, laughter still creasing his lips. "It embarrasses you to hear such things?"

"No," she admitted. "Though it might if one of my own countrymen tried the same lines."

"The English are men of action," came the dry comment. "They waste neither time nor breath on words."

Considering her somewhat limited experience, Chelsea was in no position to personally confirm or deny the truth in that statement, though the men she had got as far as kissing in the past certainly hadn't been all that verbose.

"Perhaps they should take lessons from the Greeks," she said, tongue-in-cheek. "Although, aren't the French supposed to be the best lovers?"

She squealed as Nikos rolled her over to administer a smart slap.

"That," he said, "is for your impudence. The French are not in the same league."

Chelsea pulled a face at him. "That was taking an unfair advantage!"

"It was indeed," he agreed imperturbably. "An excuse to lay my hand on a particularly delightful portion of your anatomy."

She had to laugh herself; it was impossible not to. "You're incorrigible!" she accused.

"That, and more. If we're going to stay here a time longer, you should put more lotion on your skin."

Chelsea sat up with reluctance to reach for the bottle from her soft leather bag, only to have it taken from her.

"I'll apply it to your back, where you can't reach for yourself," Nikos stated. "Lie down again."

She obeyed without argument, aware of the glint in his eyes and the increase in her pulse-rate. If this was another excuse to lay hands on her, she was all for it!

The coldness of the liquid he poured between her shoulderblades brought a gasp to her lips, the suppleness of the fingers smoothing it over her skin a spreading warmth and languor. Head resting on her bent arms, she drifted in a sea of pure pleasure as he worked down the length of her back. If it were only possible, she thought dreamily, to freeze these moments the way a camera froze an image, to be taken out later and recalled in every detail.

She came down to earth with reluctance when he finished, avoiding his gaze as she sat up to do the rest. There was no halting time. Those moments were gone for ever.

They stayed on the island until the sun was halfway down the sky. By the time they set sail for home, Dimitris was too weary to keep his eyes open. Chelsea put him to bed in one of the two cabins, then made coffee in the well-equipped galley.

It would be possible to live full-time on a boat like this, she mused. Enjoyable too. Not that Nikos was likely to consider it, of course. His home was on Skalos, his commitments too pressing. Perhaps one day, when he had had enough of the business world, he might indulge in a voyage to far distant lands, but she wouldn't be with him.

She took the coffee up on deck, surprised and a not a little perturbed to see the ominous darkness looming astern.

"Squall coming," Nikos confirmed. "We shan't reach Skalos before it breaks, I'm afraid."

Chelsea felt her spirits sink. Faced with the increased motion as the *Aphrodite* breasted the rising waves, her sea legs were already starting to give up on her. It would be just her luck to get sick!

She wasn't, though it was touch and go. Nikos insisted she go below again when the rain came sweeping across in a solid sheet. It had passed inside twenty minutes or so, and the sun was shining once more when she ven-

tured back on deck to find him soaked to the skin, his
hair a mass of glistening raindrops.

Anticipating that, she had a towel all ready, watching
as he rubbed at the black pelt. He had taken off the white
shirt in order to wring it out; she could see muscle ripple
beneath the olive skin as he moved. Another image to
recall—except that memory was no substitute for reality.

On impulse, she went to him, running the tips of her
fingers down the line of his spinal column and pressing
her lips to the firm flesh. She heard his soft exclamation,
felt the vibration through his frame. There might be a
time when he no longer reacted to her touch this way,
but it certainly wasn't yet. There was comfort in that.

It was gone six when they dropped anchor in the cove.
Bright-eyed and bushy-tailed again after his sleep,
Dimitris was reluctant for the day to end. Bedtime would
have to be put back a little if he was to sleep at all,
Chelsea reckoned as they drove back to the house.

The three of them went indoors together—like any
family returning from a day out. Chelsea had donned a
pair of tailored shorts and a crisp white shirt over her
bikini, but she felt stripped naked by the fleeting, con-
temptuous gaze of the woman who emerged from the
saloni.

Superb body clad in what was obviously a designer
dress in two-tone greens, her glossy black hair scooped
up from a face fit to grace any magazine cover, she was
a sight to set any man's pulses racing. Certainly she
stopped Nikos dead in his tracks.

He addressed her in Greek, surprising Chelsea
with the curtness of his tone. She caught the name
Marguerite.

Apparently somewhat taken aback herself, the newcomer answered on a note that sounded more placatory

than angry to Chelsea's ears. Whilst she was unable to understand the words themselves, she had a sudden, heart-sinking notion of what they might be about. This woman was Nikos's mainland mistress, here uninvited and facing his displeasure because of it.

"I'll take Dimitris upstairs, shall I?" she said expressionlessly.

Nikos glanced her way, brows drawn, mouth set like a trap. "Do," was all he said.

"Perhaps you might introduce me to your visitor first," she suggested, resenting the summary dismissal.

For a moment she thought he might refuse, then he nodded brusquely. "Marguerite Alexandros—Chelsea Lovatt."

Chelsea gave the other woman a deliberated smile. *"Khero poli."*

There was no answering smile, just a look of disdain and a brief response. Dimitris tugged at Chelsea's hand, obviously eager to be gone from an atmosphere he could sense if not understand.

They left the two of them standing there and mounted the stairs. Chelsea felt as if her heart was stuck in the pit of her stomach. Prepared though she had been to believe that Nikos had some kind of set-up in Athens, it was something else again to have the proof of it thrust in her face. She was making no mistake, for sure. Marguerite Alexandros was the woman who had rung here last night when he got back—the woman he had left to come straight to her.

"Why does Papa not want the lady to be here?" asked Dimitris curiously. "He said she should not have come."

"Perhaps he just doesn't care for unexpected visitors," Chelsea answered carefully. "I think you should have your bath before supper tonight. That looks like oil on your foot."

"It was on some of the rocks," he said, successfully sidetracked. "Papa says it comes from the big ships when they clean out their tanks ill—" His brow knitted as he sought the word. "When it is wrong?"

"Illegally," Chelsea supplied. "Never mind, a good scrub in hot soapy water will get rid of it."

From the look on the small face, the prospect wasn't enticing. Splashing around in a rock pool was one thing, sitting in a bathtub quite another.

Clean and fed, he was asleep within minutes of going to bed at eight. Chelsea took a shower, and got into the blue tunic dress, viewing her reflection in the cheval mirror with lack-lustre eyes. She had seen nothing of either Nikos or his lady-friend in the past couple of hours. Nor did she want to see them. The very thought of sitting at dinner with this Marguerite across the table was anathema to her.

It was over between her and Nikos. It had to be. Suspecting that there were other women in his life was one thing, having it proven was another. Having met this Marguerite, there was no way she would ever be able to close out the images of the two of them together: Nikos kissing that red mouth, caressing that voluptuous body, murmuring the words that sprang so easily to his lips.

She delayed going down until ten minutes to the hour, disconcerted to find Nikos alone in the *saloni*.

"I apologise for the intrusion," he said without preamble. "It won't be happening again."

"What did you do?" asked Chelsea with deliberated flippancy. "Send her to bed without any supper?"

"I sent her back to where she belongs," he returned. "She should not have come."

"On the grounds that you prefer to keep your women separate?"

He observed her dispassionately. "I own *no* woman."

"Just use whichever one happens to be available!" She had meant to stay cool, calm and in control, but the words formed themselves. "She's your mistress, isn't she? The permanent one as opposed to the temporary!"

There was no change in his expression. "You consider yourself merely used?"

The anger went out of her suddenly, leaving her defenceless against the pain. "All right, it takes two," she said thickly. "I didn't have to go along. I suppose I'm just not cut out for this kind of situation."

Standing, hands thrust into trouser pockets, gaze unrevealing, Nikos said levelly, "What are you telling me?"

Trust him to cut to the bottom line, Chelsea thought. She drew a steadying breath. "I think it's time I moved on."

"You promised to stay until I found a replacement for Ledra. Would you punish Dimitris for my sins?"

"That's emotional blackmail," she accused, and saw a faint smile touch the firm lips.

"Call it what you will. You gave your word."

"That was...before."

"You knew what was to happen between us. It was always inevitable. And in no way were you naive enough to believe me living a life of celibacy up until then."

"It isn't celibacy, or the lack of it, that bothers me," she got out. "I just don't like the idea of you coming to me direct from her yesterday."

The dark brows drew together. "You believe that's what I did?"

"You're saying it isn't?" she asked after a moment.

"Yes."

The simple affirmative carried more weight than any amount of indignant denial. Chelsea gazed at him in emotional confusion.

"Even so, you wouldn't deny that she *is* your mistress?"

His shoulders lifted in a brief shrug. "We have no formal arrangement."

"But you do take care of her financially?"

"She has an income of her own sufficient to her needs." There was a hint of intolerance now in the tone of his voice, a spark in the dark eyes. "Am I to be catechised any further?"

Chelsea bit her lip, recognising his right to be annoyed by her persistence. She was in no position to stand in judgement of his lifestyle; she was in no position to stand in judgement of anyone!

"I'm sorry," she said stiffly. "I'm being presumptuous. I just don't like the thought of being involved in a *ménage à trois,* that's all."

"For that," Nikos responded on a dry note, "Marguerite would have to be living here. This was the first time she ever set foot on Skalos." He paused, expression unrevealing as he studied her face. "Would she have taken it into her head to make the journey at all had I paid her recent attention, do you think?"

Eyes brilliant as they attempted to pierce the inscrutable façade, Chelsea said slowly, "I suppose not."

"She came," he continued in the same unemotional tones, "because I've neglected to contact her in any way during the past week. My mind, it could be said, has been on other matters."

She gazed at him, wanting so badly to believe him,

yet at the same time wondering what difference it made in the long run. There was no permanency in their relationship.

Nikos resolved the immediate dilemma himself by coming to take her forcefully into his arms. It crossed her mind to resist, but only for a second. She was building up more and more heartache for the future, she knew, but this was now, and she was weak.

"Do you still wish to leave?" he asked softly some minutes later.

Head resting against the broad chest, Chelsea couldn't find enough will-power to raise an eyebrow, much less make any momentous decisions. "Not right this moment, at any rate," she murmured.

"That's good, because I'm not prepared to let you go right this moment."

Only when he was good and ready, she surmised. By which time she had to be the same herself.

"You have my word," he added on the same soft note, "that while ever we are together, the two of us, there will be no other."

She believed him, because he had taken the trouble to say it when he could quite easily have left her to think what she might. It was worth a great deal to her just to have that much.

The following twenty-four hours were blissful in every respect. They took the *Aphrodite* out again, calling at the neighbouring islet to explore the tiny ruined chapel before heading out to sea for the day. Chelsea learned how to handle the yacht, at least in calm waters; she even learned how to reef a sail. She was an apt pupil and Nikos praised her, obviously pleased by her readiness to take an active part.

Another string to her bow, she reflected. Not that she

was likely to have much opportunity to further her maritime education once she was home again.

She shut off that train of thought determinedly. Home was where the heart was, and right now that was here.

With the father he so obviously worshipped on hand, Dimitris was in his seventh heaven. Chelsea loved to listen to the two of them discuss matters she was sure would never have crossed her mind as a five-year-old. She was able to contribute herself on occasion, once by explaining how the magazine Dimitris had been looking at was produced.

"You've been involved in such work at some time?" asked Nikos.

There was no note of suspicion in his voice, but it brought her up with a jerk nevertheless. If ever there was a time for telling him the truth, it was now, but she couldn't bring herself to take it for fear of his reaction. Deception was deception, whichever way one wrapped it up.

"No," she said, plumping for a half-truth instead. "Just something I picked up. You're a mine of information," she added, hoping to turn the spotlight away. "A veritable encyclopedia, in fact!"

"You give me too much credit," he responded easily. "There are many things I know nothing about at all."

Love being one of them, came the thought, hastily despatched before it could weigh too heavily.

This time when they returned home, there was no Marguerite to greet them. Instead they found a man awaiting them. Although he was some twenty years or so older than Nikos, there was enough of a resemblance between the two of them for Chelsea to guess who the other was. He wasted no time in polite salutations, but

launched into a tirade that brought a dark frown to
Nikos's face.

"It seems that Dion has taken Elini from the island,"
he explained, for Chelsea's benefit.

"To where?" she asked, nonplussed.

"That," he said, "no one appears to know."

"You were the one who urged my son to make this
union, were you not?" demanded the other man
brusquely. "You knew of his intentions!"

"I suggested he make his feelings clear to Elini,"
Chelsea admitted. "I didn't realise at the time that they
wouldn't be welcomed by her family. And no, I had no
idea he had this in mind. I haven't even seen him for
days."

That he didn't believe her was evident. If his expression was anything to go by, he was ready to force the
information from her by physical means if necessary.
She took an involuntary half-step backwards, and felt
Nikos's arm come about her shoulders, stopping her
from moving further.

"If Chelsea says she has no knowledge of Dion's intentions, then you must accept it, Kanaris," he stated
unequivocally. "Steps must be taken to find the two of
them before any further harm is done. How long have
they been gone?"

His uncle answered in Greek, but Chelsea was able to
work out that the pair had been missing since around
one o'clock that afternoon. In four hours they could be
far away!

"I'll contact the authorities and have a watch put on
all ports," said Nikos. "It's possible that they already
landed, of course, in which case the search will be extended inland. They *will* be found," he emphasised
grimly, "you can be assured of that!"

Whether the other was or not, he acknowledged the assertion with an inclination of his head, and departed.

"Why is it your place to do all the running around?" Chelsea asked diffidently as Nikos removed the protective arm from her shoulders. "Surely it should be up to the two fathers to get together—if that's the way it has to be at all!"

Nikos gave her a narrowed glance. "You see the situation through the eyes of a romantic, with no thought for anyone but the two of them. There is every possibility that the suitor Thannasis has chosen for his daughter will no longer be available if her good name is put in doubt."

"In which case, why not accept things the way they are and allow her to marry Dion?"

He made a small, impatient gesture. "As I said before, he has no means of supporting a wife."

"He could have," she insisted, "if you provided him with a job. I know he's shown no interest in working for a living up to now," she went on swiftly, before Nikos could voice the dissension she could see in his eyes, "but he'd see things differently now, I'm sure."

"Then you're more certain than I," came the brusque response. "You've known Dion only a few days. You can have little idea of his true nature."

"In other words, I'm to keep my nose out of it!" she flashed. "Why don't you just say it straight?"

"Very well." The glitter in the dark eyes bespoke an anger threatening to spill over if much more pressure was applied. "You will leave the matter to those whose business it is!"

About to rush into ill-considered response, Chelsea caught a sudden glimpse of a small pinched face, and felt fury give way to shame. Dropping to her knees, she hugged Dimitris to her, thankful to feel his arms creep about her neck.

"It's all right," she murmured. "Just two silly grown-ups having a disagreement. It's over now."

He took a peep at his father, as if in doubt of that statement, obviously reassured enough by what he saw to form a wavery smile. "You were speaking very loudly!"

"I'm sorry, Dimitris." Nikos sounded as if he really meant it. "I was wrong to raise my voice to Chelsea."

"I asked for it," she said, forcing herself to look him in the eye as she straightened. "You were right, none of this is my business."

He inclined his head expressionlessly. "I could have found less hurtful words."

"But they'd still have meant the same thing."

"Basically, yes. Our ways are not your ways."

Nor ever could be. He didn't have to put that message into words; she already knew it. The anger was still there in him; she knew that too. No foreigner—and especially not a female foreigner—could be allowed to question his beliefs.

"Dimitris and I will go on up, if you want to get on with turning out the search parties," she said, with what composure she could muster. "See you at dinner."

She didn't have to wait that long. He joined the two of them some twenty minutes later.

"We leave for Athens within the next hour," he announced without preamble.

Chelsea stared at him, wondering if she had misunderstood. "We?" she queried.

"The three of us," he confirmed, drawing a shout of delight from his son and a brief smile to his own lips. "My time will be taken tomorrow, but after that I hope to be free again. Do you require any assistance in packing?''

"I can manage," she said, trying not to let elation overcome practicality. "I don't have all that much choice myself." She hesitated, searching the strong features. "Are you sure you want us along?"

He looked back at her with a certain cynicism. "I'm not in the habit of saying things I don't mean to say. It's time Dimitris saw something of the world outside of Skalos. Tomorrow, the two of you can take in the sights. You know Athens at all?"

"Only superficially." Chelsea hesitated, reluctant to mar the moment. "Do you have any news of Dion and Elini?"

He shook his head, mouth taking on the intractable line that warned her not to pursue the subject any further. "The helicopter will be here in fifty minutes."

Chelsea took the hint. She was going to get nothing more out of him; that was certain. She could only hope that the two runaways would be accorded at least a little sympathy and understanding when they were found. That they would be found she didn't doubt for a moment. Nikos would leave no stone unturned.

CHAPTER ELEVEN

NOSE pressed to the window, Dimitris relished every minute of the helicopter journey. This was adventure with a capital A! Chelsea thought sea travel preferable any day of the week.

As neither Dimitris nor his father gave any indication of alarm during the taxi ride into the city, she concluded that she had to be the only one finding both the pace and the traffic hair-raising. Like the French, drivers here were all throttle and brake with horn accompaniment!

The luxury apartment block at the foot of Lycabettus was in total contrast to the simplicity of the villa back on Skalos, the penthouse suite breathtaking in design and decor.

"Why on earth would you need three bedrooms?" Chelsea asked Nikos bemusedly, following an excited Dimitris back to the vast, superbly furnished living area.

"It was designed with three bedrooms," he said, as if that answered everything. "Perhaps fortunately so, as there are three of us here now. One mine, and one each for you and Dimitris."

Meeting the dark eyes, Chelsea wished she had kept her mouth shut. "I meant normally," she said. "It all seems a bit much after Skalos."

Nikos eyed her speculatively. "Most women would prefer to spend their time here."

"Some, perhaps," she contradicted. "Not all. It's superb, I admit, but it lacks...soul."

He laughed, not in the least put out. "I'll pass on that

155

message to the architect. You might approve of the roof
garden. We'll be eating dinner there tonight.''

"I too?" asked Dimitris anxiously. "I'm very hungry!''

Lips twitching, his father nodded. "As a special treat
you may join us. But only,'' he added with mock severity, "if you behave yourself."

"He always behaves himself," Chelsea put in. "Unlike some I could mention." It was only on catching the
quizzical glance that she realised the possible misinterpretation of the remark. "I meant my sister's boys," she
added hurriedly.

"Who else?" Nikos sounded amused. "Perhaps
you'd like to unpack your things while I order dinner
from the service restaurant. Yours will be the second
room on the right.''

Which put her conveniently next door to the room she
had already identified as his. Would he expect her to go
to him tonight, she wondered hungrily, or would he
come to her? Always providing she wasn't taking too
much for granted all round, of course.

The views from every room were tremendous. As
darkness descended over the city, lights began springing to life, outlining the incomparable shape of the
Parthenon in the middle distance. There was a Sound
and Light pageant every night throughout the summer,
Chelsea believed. The effects would be clearly visible
from here. Nice to see on occasion, she supposed, but
she would still rather be back on Skalos.

She sorted Dimitris out first, leaving him playing happily with his beloved pinball game while she went to
look through her own things for something to wear for
the evening. Not for the first time this last week, she
deplored the limitations of her wardrobe. Nikos had seen

her in everything. Out of everything too, if it came to that.

Perhaps she might find time to do a little shopping tomorrow while he was tied up. Nothing fancy; she couldn't run to designer wear. Dimitris wouldn't mind visiting a shop or two, she was sure. It would all be part and parcel of this wonderful new experience.

An oasis of greenery, unaffected by traffic fumes this far above the busy streets, the roof garden belonged wholly to the penthouse suite. Chelsea couldn't even begin to imagine what a place like this must have cost. To someone in Nikos's position, she supposed the question was irrelevant. It was probably tax deductible anyway.

The *son et lumière* began as they were finishing the meal brought to them in a heated trolley. Sitting there, with the man and boy she loved, watching the sweeping lights and listening to the distant sounds, Chelsea felt a welling happiness. Whatever happened in the future, no one could ever take such moments away from her.

Worn out with all the excitement, Dimitris nodded off. Chelsea got up to scoop him from the chair, shaking her head as Nikos made to rise himself.

"You stay and finish your coffee," she said. "This is what I'm here for."

"Not entirely," he answered, with a glint that played havoc on her heartstrings. "The night is still young."

He came to find her when she failed to return to the roof after putting Dimitris to bed, sweeping her up from the chair where she had settled herself to watch the rest of the light show.

"This," he declared purposefully, "is *not* what I had in mind for your entertainment tonight!"

"Actually," she answered with demure expression, "it isn't what *I* had in mind for yours."

Laughter curved the firm lips, sparkling in his eyes. "Then we're of the same mind, *yineka!*"

If only! she thought as he bore her across to the door.

He was gone when she woke at six. With Dimitris in the apartment she had expected nothing else, but she still felt bereft. Lying there, she visualised what it would be like to waken with him still by her side—to rouse him to make love to her in the early-morning light. If she knew him at all, he would need no encouragement. As he had said last night, in that way they were of one mind.

Seated at a table set within the curve of the huge window, Nikos was finishing his usual light breakfast of coffee and the hoop-shaped biscuits called *koulouria* when she went through to the living room. The separate dining room would be kept for formal entertaining, Chelsea assumed. The table in there would comfortably seat a dozen or more.

"Do you have far to go?" she asked, taking a seat herself and reaching for the coffee pot.

"How far would you like me to go?" he rejoined equably.

Chelsea cast him a quelling glance. "I meant to the office, as you well know!"

"Perhaps my grasp of your language isn't quite as comprehensive as you think," he said.

"Perhaps pigs might fly!" she snorted, adding hastily, "And don't take *that* the wrong way!"

The dark eyes glinted at her. "This time it wasn't applied personally. Not that I find your colloquialisms easy on the ear at any time. If I hear Dimitris using one, I'll—"

"Come down on me like a ton of bricks!" she supplied straight-faced, drawing one of the rare boyish grins.

"It would take a great deal more than that, I think, to flatten you." He glanced at his watch, took a last gulp of coffee and pushed back his chair. "I must go. The board is sitting at eight."

"And it would hardly do for the company president to be late," she quipped, wishing he didn't have to leave at all.

She knew some consolation when he rounded the table with the obvious intention of delivering a parting kiss, even more when he hauled her to her feet to do it properly.

"This evening we spend alone," he said. "Dimitris will be taken care of. There will be a car at your disposal whenever you're ready to leave. *Adio, yineka.*"

He was gone before she could find an adequate response, leaving her to face a long, long day without him. She had Dimitris, though. That in itself was enough to cheer her up. They were going to have a great time together, the two of them!

They did. Driven by a middle-aged man named Costas—a name as often given in Greece as John in England—they toured the city, stopping off where and when the mood took them. Dimitris was fascinated by everything he saw, voluble in his curiosity. Chelsea had to resort to a guide-book in order to answer many of his questions.

Mindful of the fact that many shops even in the city observed siesta from two-thirty until five, she took the opportunity to visit one or two in the vicinity of the restaurant where they ate lunch. Dimitris helped her out with the language where an English-speaking assistant couldn't be found, acquiring a regular fan club in the process.

He also voiced a very definite opinion of the things she tried on, shaking his head emphatically at a bright yellow sarong she donned purely as a joke. Not her colour, he declared, with an authority that reminded Chelsea so much of his father she could barely keep her face straight.

She finished up with three dresses that met with his approval, plus a couple of pairs of shoes that met with hers. He'd shown no dissension when she'd tentatively mentioned the plan for the evening, just expressed the hope that the person who stayed with him would be able to play Hangman.

It was when they were emerging from the last shop that they spotted Dion—at least Dimitris did. He was standing outside a shop across the road, and seemingly alone. Chelsea made a frantic grab for the boy as he started forward, missing him by inches. She watched in horror as he darted between the traffic streams, offering up a heartfelt prayer of thanks when by some miracle he reached the far side without mishap.

Ignoring the imprecations cast her way by irate drivers she forced to pull up by simply stepping out, holding up the bags containing her purchases, she made the far pavement herself. Dimitris hung his head when she remonstrated with him, unaccustomed to her anger.

"Ilikrina lipame," he said in subdued tones, too upset to remember to speak English.

"He says he's really sorry," Dion translated. "Just be thankful he's safe."

Chelsea gave him a fierce look. "I am. That doesn't mean turning a blind eye to what might have happened. Nikos—"

"Nikos isn't with you," he returned flatly. "Dimitris already told me that. I suppose you're going to tell him you saw me?"

Chelsea hesitated. "If I don't, Dimitris will."

"Not if we both ask him not to do so." There was a

look almost of pleading in the dark eyes. "Elini is in there," he said, indicating the shop at his back, "buying a dress for our wedding. Once the marriage has taken place, no one can part us."

"There are people out searching for the two of you," she said. "It must be known by now that you're here in Athens."

He shook his head. "We landed on Evia, and came by bus and ferry. By the time our steps are traced, it will be too late."

"How will you live?" asked Chelsea dubiously. "You don't even have a job."

"I could have one, if Nikos was to be persuaded of my will to work."

A very big "if" indeed! she thought, recalling Nikos's response to her own suggestion.

Reading the expression in her eyes, Dion shrugged philosophically. "As you would say yourself, it's early days as yet, and my mother will always support me."

"She may not have a choice if your father refuses to allow it."

"If that happened, I'd go to the newspapers and spill the beans." He used the slang term with hardy deliberation. "Nikos would be loath to have Pandrossos affairs made common knowledge—especially if it also came out that his English paramour isn't wholly what she appears to be."

Chelsea drew in a steadying breath, glancing down at Dimitris, who fortunately appeared to be engrossed in watching the traffic. "Is that a threat?" she asked, low-toned.

Dion looked faintly ashamed. "No. I'd gain nothing from exposing you." He paused, the plea evident once more. "All I ask is that you tell no one you've seen me here."

"I can't ask Dimitris to lie," she said.

"I can." He squatted to bring himself on a level with his young cousin, drawing his attention. He spoke in Greek, summoning first puzzlement to the small face, then a somewhat reluctant compliance.

"No one," he repeated, straightening again. "Please, Chelsea!"

Although hating the idea of involving Dimitris in the deception, she couldn't bring herself to turn him down. He had to love Elini to distraction in order to go to such ends. Her feelings for him must run as deep too, for her to be prepared to defy her father. A romantic viewpoint, perhaps, but what was life without a little romance?

"All right," she agreed, with some reluctance still. "Just make sure you don't let Elini down, that's all."

For what she could do about it if he did, it was a bit of a pointless caution, but he appeared to take it to heart.

"Will you go before Elini sees you?" he urged. "It's best that she believes us safe from discovery still."

Costas was to pick them up at the end of the street at two-thirty. It was twenty-five minutes past the hour now. Chelsea made an effort to infuse genuine heartiness into her voice. "Good luck to you both!"

She took Dimitris's unresisting hand in her free one and started out along the thronged pavement. He stayed silent until they reached the limousine already waiting for them at the kerbside, then seemed to cast off any possible disturbance of mind. Chelsea wished she could only do the same. Facing Nikos knowing what she knew was going to be difficult, to say the least. She would just have to hope that Dion's name wouldn't be mentioned.

They were back in the apartment by three, to find that Nikos hadn't yet returned. After settling Dimitris for an afternoon nap, Chelsea retired to her own room with the intention of doing the same herself, but found sleep difficult to come by. She had two secrets now. If Nikos discovered either, they would be finished. She hesitated to think what his reaction might be to the discovery of his son's involvement in the latter deception.

She must have dozed off eventually, opening her eyes to see Nikos sitting on the bed-edge watching her.

"You look so defenceless asleep," he said softly. "The tigress becomes a kitten again."

"Tigresses have cubs, not kittens," she murmured, mind not yet back in full gear. "And cubs still have claws and teeth."

The smile came slow and meaningful. "I wouldn't have them drawn."

Chelsea slid both arms about his neck as he found her lips with his, cherishing the possessiveness of the hand seeking her breast. She had taken off her outer clothing before lying down, and was wearing only a brief lacy bra and panties. Memory chose the moment he began removing them to return with full force, causing her heart to drop like a stone, her body to stiffen involuntarily beneath his hands.

Nikos lifted his head to look at her questioningly, the line between his brows deepening as he studied her face. "What is it?" he asked. "Did I hurt you?"

She shook her head, struggling to stay on top of her conscience. "Dimitris," she said. "He'll be awake by now. He may come in."

The frown cleared. "True. I'd forgotten." He made to rise. "I'll lock the door."

"No!" Chelsea caught herself up as he turned back to look at her with brows drawn once more. "What's he going to think if he finds it locked and hears you in here with me?"

For a moment, Nikos kept the same penetrating gaze on her, expression hard to define, then he lifted his shoulders in a resigned shrug. "You're right, of course. This is not the time."

Chelsea knew an urge to reach out and clutch him back to her as he got to his feet. She resisted it by sheer effort of will. Nikos was no fool. It was going to be necessary to exercise a great deal of care if he wasn't to suspect that she was hiding something from him.

The woman he'd hired to look after Dimitris arrived at seven-thirty. She was in her forties, and spoke little English, but she looked a whole lot more fun than Ledra. Allowed to stay up for an extra hour or so again, Dimitris lost little time in introducing her to the joys of Hangman. When Chelsea and Nikos left at eight, the two of them were already deeply into the game.

"She'd be very suitable to replace Ledra, don't you think?" Chelsea ventured as they descended in the lift.

Nikos shook his head. "She has family of her own here in Athens."

"But you are looking for someone?" she insisted, giving the screw a masochistic turn.

He angled a narrowed regard. "It takes time. You promised me a month."

"You've got it," she said swiftly, assured of that much at least. "I'm in no hurry."

The hard-boned features relaxed again. "Good." He ran his eyes down the length of her in the form-fitting little black dress that had cost her an arm and a good half of a leg, lifting them to dwell on the face-framing golden mane she had spent an hour washing and brushing into shining obedience. "Every man who sees you tonight will want you," he declared with heart-stirring extravagance. "But only I will have the privilege of fulfilling that desire. I can barely wait for the moment."

He wasn't on his own, she thought, feeling her knees

go wobbly. For the first time in her life she actually wished for a lift to break down!

They took the same limousine they had used during the day, this time with a different driver. Seated in the darkened rear, drawn close to Nikos's side, Chelsea shut out any thought of the future. It was enough to be here with him now, feeling the muscular power of the arm about her shoulders—knowing she stirred him the same way he stirred her. It might not be love on his part, but it was the very next best thing.

The evening began with drinks in the Rendezvous bar of the Grande Bretagne hotel, from where they moved on eventually to a nightclub on the twenty-fourth floor of a palatial high-rise that was obviously one of the "in" places to be in modern Athens.

The name Pandrossos brought immediate and defer-ential attention, with the *maître d'* himself waiting on their table. The focus of several pairs of eyes in the immediate vicinity, Chelsea felt like a microbe under a microscope, although Nikos seemed not to notice the interest they were drawing. The fact that she was English would be causing speculation, of course.

A superbly presented floor show was followed by dancing for those in the mood. Held close against the broad chest, Chelsea could feel the steady beat of Nikos's heart beneath the white tuxedo that set off his striking dark looks to such effect. Steadier than hers, for sure.

"Happy?" he asked softly, looking down into her face.

"Ecstatic" was the word that came most readily to mind, but it seemed a bit too over the top. She opted for flippancy instead. "You certainly know how to give a girl a good time, *kirie!*"

His smile was slow, curling her insides. "The night is not yet over."

It was certainly getting on that way. Not wearing a watch herself, Chelsea peered round his shoulder to try reading the one on a male wrist close by, almost jumping out of her skin in surprise when the owner of the wrist addressed her by name.

Her spirits plummeted as she lifted her eyes to the face above. Of all the places in the world, of all the nights in a year, why did someone like Paul Johnson have to choose these same two?

"I had to check it was really you," he said.

Nikos turned so that he could see who had spoken, drawing an expression Chelsea recognised only too well to the other man's face. Until this moment he obviously hadn't been too certain of her partner's identity either, but he was now.

"Will you not introduce us?" said Nikos on a formal note.

"Paul Johnson—Nikos Pandrossos," she murmured, mind searching desperately for a way out, and finding none. She forced herself to smile at the attractive brunette in Paul's arms. "Hi, there!"

"Diane Rossiter—Chelsea Lovatt," Paul completed, borrowing her style. The pale blue eyes were shrewd as they rested on her face. "Some coincidence running into you like this so far from home!"

"Isn't it?" Chelsea couldn't think of another thing to say. Her cover was about to be blown, and she couldn't do a thing about it. She could feel Nikos glance at her—sense the narrowing of his eyes.

"We're causing an obstruction, standing here this way in the centre of the floor," he said. "Perhaps you would care to join us at our table for a drink?"

Paul wasted no time asking his companion's opinion. "That's very civil of you. We'd be delighted."

A temporary reprieve only, Chelsea acknowledged

hollowly as the four of them made their way from the floor. Freelance like herself, Paul Johnson had a nose like a bloodhound when it came to scenting a story. There was no way he was going to let this one go.

Nikos ordered brandies all round from the waiter who materialised as if by magic at his elbow the moment he regained his seat at the table. He appeared completely relaxed, but Chelsea knew the keenness of the mind behind that suave exterior. He had picked up on the vibes out there for sure.

"Are you in Athens on business or vacation?" he asked Paul.

Chelsea held her breath, waiting for the axe to fall. The word "journalist" alone would probably be enough to set him putting two and two together. If she had only admitted it from the start, along with her decision not to pursue any story, she would have had nothing to fear, but he was hardly likely to take her word now.

"Oh, purely vacation," Paul answered easily, affording her yet another reprieve. "A few days here, then we're off down to Crete. Diane's brother runs a bar in Agios Nikolaos. Making a success of it too, apparently. Even the locals patronise it."

Nikos looked suitably impressed. "He's been there how long?"

Diane elected to answer that herself. "Three years. He married a Greek girl the same year he opened, which helped, I suppose."

"It certainly won't have done him any harm," Nikos agreed, turning a smile that brought a sudden sparkle to her eyes. "You propose helping in the bar while you're there?"

She laughed. "Do you think the locals would object if I did?"

"I'm sure your presence would prove an even greater draw."

Chelsea had every sympathy with the other girl's obvious response. Coming from Nikos, even the trite had impact. Diane was maybe a year or two older than herself, which brought her within a couple of years of Paul. They made an attractive pair, she had to admit.

Paul had been with *World* when she'd first gone to work there. They had dated a couple of times, but she hadn't been interested in progressing the relationship, and apart from the odd occasion in the course of work they'd lost touch. Having him turn up like this was pure bad luck—or could it be called poetic justice?

"So how long have *you* been in Athens, then?" queried the subject of her thoughts, jerking her out of them.

"We arrived only yesterday," said Nikos, before she could gather herself to reply.

The pale blue eyes were alight with curiosity. "From where?"

It was obvious from his expression that the older man found the question intrusive, but he answered with what Chelsea considered remarkable restraint. "From my home on Skalos. Chelsea has been taking care of my small son."

"Really?" The interest was deepening by the second. "I didn't realise you'd gone in for nannying, Chelsea."

"A temporary arrangement," Nikos cut in smoothly again. "Until a nurse can be found who meets my requirements."

"Is your son with you?" asked Diane. "In Athens, I mean," she added with a laugh. "I'd hardly expect you to have brought him here, of course!"

"Hardly," echoed Nikos drily. "Yes, he's in Athens. Asleep in his bed at the moment, it would be hoped."

"How old is he?"

"Just five years."

"Oh, how lovely! I adore children that age—especially little boys. They're so utterly cute!"

If she laid it on any thicker she would bury them all! thought Chelsea in disgust, momentarily distracted. She glanced at Nikos, unsurprised to see the faint curl at the corners of his lips.

"They are indeed," he rejoined.

There was a brief silence. Chelsea could almost feel Paul's mind ticking over, seeking a means of extending the conversation into yet more personal detail. What puzzled her was that Nikos himself had made no attempt as yet to ask how she and Paul knew one another. If it came to that, Paul was being pretty cagey too.

But then, he would be, wouldn't he? He'd be as aware as she had been that Nikos Pandrossos had no great regard for the press in any shape or form. Her involvement with the shipping tycoon was icing on the cake so far as he was concerned: what he would make of it, given the opportunity, she hesitated to think. Ethics played little part in his professional life. One of the reasons they had never hit it off.

There was only one way out of the mess she had landed herself in, and that was to come clean, she decided fatalistically. Here and now, for preference, before Paul could gain any further advantage.

She drew in a shaky breath before taking the plunge, knowing what the outcome was likely to be. "I think you should take warning, Nikos," she said. "Paul is a journalist too."

CHAPTER TWELVE

THE blanking out of all expression from the hard-featured face was in its way more daunting than any invective. Nikos kept his eyes fixed on the man opposite, but Chelsea knew the full message had got through.

"I'm off duty!" Paul protested, recognising a blow-out when he saw it coming.

"Journalists are never off duty," came the controlled response. "You will excuse us."

Chelsea got to her feet along with him. She was going to be facing the music in private; she had expected that. Now, or later, it was going to make little difference in the long run. In Nikos's eyes she had infiltrated his home under false pretences. The deception wouldn't be taken lightly.

Thwarted of his prey, Paul turned ugly, as she had known he would. "Seems you learned to use your advantages at last," he sneered. "Hope it proves worth it!"

Chelsea felt Nikos's hand come under her elbow in a bruising grip, turning her from the table. She fixed a smile to her face as he urged her forward, aware of eyes other than Paul's and Diane's following the two of them. Paul might not have got all the personal detail he had hoped for, but he would use what he did have to best effect; there was nothing surer. Nikos would know that too.

No word passed between them in the lift. Chelsea was too demoralised to even attempt an explanation. She caught her heel on the edge of the marble step as they exited from the building, to be hauled upright without ceremony. There was every chance that the stumble had been judged as another ruse of hers to gain sympathy, she thought ruefully as she was put into the limousine that somehow appeared at just the right moment.

With the glass slider between passenger and driver compartments closed, she expected the inquisition to commence immediately, but Nikos remained silent, face moulded in bronze under the street lighting. She said his name tentatively, to be frozen into muteness again by the glittering glance he turned on her. The anger was almost tangible.

It was gone one o'clock when they reached the apartment. Chelsea went to check on Dimitris, while Nikos despatched the sitter to the car he had kept waiting. He was standing at the wide window when she returned to the living room, a glass in hand.

"So?" he said without turning.

So what? was the first response that sprang to mind; one hardly scheduled to keep the cart on the wheels, she had to admit. "It isn't the way it might seem," she substituted.

He swung to look at her, starkly framed against the night sky. Non-reflective glass, came the fleeting, totally irrelevant thought.

"You're saying you're *not* a journalist yourself, after all?"

"No. I mean, yes, I'm a journalist, but—"

"But too honourable a one to contemplate publishing the material you came to obtain. Is that what you're going to tell me?"

Chelsea firmed her jaw. "Something like that, yes. I can't deny the original aim—I'd be no kind of journalist at all if I hadn't at least made the attempt. But I gave up on the idea after meeting you and realising just how slim the chances were of getting you to co-operate."

"My willing co-operation, perhaps." It was obvious from the tone that he didn't believe a word of it. "You weren't slow to recognise the attraction you had for me—nor to take advantage of it!"

"You think I deliberately injured my ankle to manipulate you into keeping me *in situ?*" she burst out fiercely. "You'll be saying next that I engineered Dimitris's accident too!"

There was the briefest of pauses as he viewed her stormy face and sparking blue eyes. "Engineered, no. A fortuitous event, in that it earned you my undying gratitude, yes. For that reason, and that reason alone, I'll grant you the interview you sought here and now—if there's anything left to tell you that you don't already know about my personal life."

"I don't want an interview." There was a hard obstruction in her throat, making speech difficult. "All I want is for you to believe me. None of what happened between us this past week has anything to do with my job. I…slept with you because I wanted to."

The firm lips twisted. "You slept with me because I gave you little choice in the matter."

"I had a choice. If I'd said no that night, you'd have accepted it."

"Could you be certain of that?"

Chelsea infused certainty into her voice now. "Yes, I could. You're no rapist, Nikos. You'd never need to be." She made a gesture of appeal. "Don't let it end like this. I give you my word that nothing you've told me will ever go any further."

He studied her with a certain cynicism. "And your contemporary back there? He also can be relied on?"

He could, she thought, biting her lip, though hardly in any helpful sense. "It's possible he'll try writing something sleazy about the two of us," she acknowledged with reluctance, "but that's not to say he'll get anyone to publish it."

From the look on Nikos's face, he was as far from believing that as she was herself. "I'm sorry," she said helplessly. "You wouldn't even have been at that place tonight if it wasn't for me."

"If you hadn't been confronted by your friend tonight, would you have told me the truth at all?" Nikos demanded.

"I don't suppose so," she admitted. "I didn't think it necessary, considering."

The dark eyes sharpened. "Considering what?"

"The fact that I'm only here on a temporary basis anyway. Three more weeks—perhaps even less, if you'd found a replacement for Ledra—and I'd have been gone." Chelsea forced a faint smile. "Why spoil things?"

Nikos made a sudden abrupt move to set down the glass he had been holding on the glass-topped table. "I think it time we retired."

She took a long, slow breath. "You're not throwing me out?"

He gave her that same cynical look. "As you said yourself, why spoil things? We still have three weeks in which to enjoy each other. We must make the most of them."

If she had any pride left at all, she would go now of her own accord, Chelsea told herself, but it did no good. Chest tight, she stood like a statue as he came towards her, trying without success to find a way in to the mind behind the hardened eyes. She made no sound when he took hold of her, closing her eyes when he brought his head down to find her mouth with his. The kiss lacked any element of tenderness, but she wasn't expecting any. All they had left was the sexual element.

"One more thing," he said as he turned her towards the door leading through to the bedrooms. "Was Dion aware of your intentions when he brought you to Skalos?"

Dion! Chelsea felt her heart miss a beat. She'd forgotten all about him! It was more a lack of courage to admit to further duplicity than reluctance to break the promise she had given which kept her from spilling it out. There was no knowing what Nikos might feel moved to do if his anger was aroused again.

"No," she said, sticking strictly to the question asked, "he wasn't."

Nikos made no further comment. He walked her past the door to his bedroom, following her into hers and closing the door behind him. Chelsea watched him take off the white tuxedo and toss it carelessly over a chair, saw the long fingers start to unbutton the smooth silk shirt.

"I don't think I want to continue with this," she said thickly. "It isn't the same."

"What difference is there?" he queried. "Are you saying you no longer want me?"

If she answered yes she would be lying through her teeth, and there had been enough of that already. She gazed at him helplessly, wishing she could turn back the clock a couple of days. Only what difference would it make anyway? The end result had never been in doubt.

"You don't trust me," she got out. "I can't blame you for that, but I can't just ignore it either. I need you to tell me you at least accept my word that I won't ever write anything about you."

He regarded her dispassionately for a lengthy moment before inclining his head. "So I accept your word."

She believed him because she believed he said nothing he didn't mean. Dion's name slid into her mind, but wasn't allowed to linger. Even if she confessed to seeing him here in Athens, there was no way of knowing his and Elini's whereabouts. By the time they were found it would probably be too late, in any case.

Lacking in deeper feeling though it might be on Nikos's side, his lovemaking was everything she had come to expect from him. He took her to the heights, leaving her limp as a rag doll in his arms, mind blanked of everything but the dreamy contentment that came with total fulfilment.

"Don't go to sleep," he said softly, looking down at her. "I haven't finished with you yet."

"Insatiable!" she murmured, and saw his lips widen a fraction.

"Is that a complaint?"

"Not on your life," she assured him, coming back to it herself as he ran the tip of his tongue over the delicate skin just behind and below her earlobe. "You're a man in a million!"

"I'm the only man you ever knew this way," he said, "so on what basis do you form that opinion?"

"Instinct." Chelsea took his face between her hands, too far gone to hide the emotions welling in her. "No other man could make me feel the way you make me feel. I love you, Nikos!"

There was no reading the expression in the dark eyes, but the irony came through loud and clear in his tone. "Of course you do."

He stopped her lips with his as she made to respond, crushing the protest before it could take form. *This* was all he wanted from her; he couldn't make that plainer. Love didn't come into it.

As always, he was gone when she opened her eyes on the morning light. Lying there, Chelsea luxuriated in the memory of their lovemaking, but reality couldn't be ousted for long. Three more weeks, if she was lucky, then goodbye to it all; the very thought tightened a steel band about her chest.

A knock on the door was followed immediately by the opening of same and a flurry of arms and legs as Dimitris flung himself across the room to leap on the bed, eyes alight with mischief.

"You have a sleep-head!" he announced.

"Are," Chelsea corrected, pulling a face at him. "And it's sleepy-head, not sleep. What time is it, anyway?"

"It is very, very late," he said.

She sat up with a jerk to look at the clock on the bedside table, shaking a fist at him when she saw it was only just gone seven. "You little monkey!"

It was only then, seeing where his eyes were riveted, that she remembered her lack of nightwear. It was odds on that he'd never seen bare breasts before this, and more than possible that Nikos wouldn't approve of him seeing them now. It was a little too late to start covering up, but nevertheless she tried.

"Why do I not have big bumps too?" he asked with interest, opening up his pyjama jacket to take a look at his own flat chest.

"Because you're a boy, and only girls have them," she said lightly. "Older girls, anyway. Why don't you go and waken your father, while I get dressed?"

"Papa is awake already." He wasn't to be sidetracked. "Why is it only girls who have them?"

"It's one way of telling the difference," she hedged. Explaining basic male/female anatomy to a five-year-old was way outside her experience. "You'd better go and get dressed yourself," she added hurriedly. "After you have a wash, of course."

"I can come under the shower with you," he suggested, bright enough to work out that where there was one difference there were likely to be others, and obviously intrigued by the idea.

"There isn't room for two of us at the same time," Chelsea claimed swiftly, which was a downright lie, as the *en suite* bathrooms were all of them equipped with shower cabinets big enough to hold a dance in. "Anyway, you don't need a shower this morning, just a facewash."

"You heard what Chelsea told you," said Nikos from the open doorway. "Go now."

Dimitris obeyed with some reluctance, breaking into laughter as his father aimed a mock slap at his rear end. Chelsea felt the colour flooding her cheeks as the dark eyes turned back her way. She had to forcibly stop herself from covering up further.

"I'm sorry," she said. "I'd forgotten I wasn't wearing anything."

He lifted a sardonic brow. "I wouldn't have imagined anything else. Dimitris had no business coming to you without permission, but there's no harm done."

"You might find he starts asking awkward questions," she mumbled, wishing he would go and wanting him to stay at one and the same time. "He wanted to know why he didn't have bumps like mine."

Still standing in the doorway, irresistible as always in white trousers and a deep green shirt, Nikos gave a short laugh. "What did you tell him?"

"Just that girls were different from boys."

"In many more ways than just the physical," came the dry response. "Some of which he'll never grasp."

"Women are no harder to fathom than men," Chelsea countered. "I never know what *you're* thinking. Well, scarcely ever, anyway," she tagged on, seeing the ironic glint. She hesitated, not sure it was the right time, but unable to let the moment pass. ''Nikos, about last night...''

''When, last night?'' he asked without particular inflexion.

''You know what I'm talking about.''

''It's dealt with,'' he said flatly. ''I've no wish to discuss the matter any further.''

''But you want me to stay?''

He observed her in silence for a moment, lips slanting as he took in every detail of her vibrant face within the tumble of bright golden hair, the smooth bare shoulders and the outline of her firmly rounded breasts.

''I'm not yet ready to let you go,'' he acknowledged, which wasn't quite what she had asked but was obviously all she was going to get. ''What would you like ordered for breakfast?''

''Coffee and *koulouria* will be fine,'' she said. ''I'm not hungry.''

He nodded. ''As you prefer.''

If only he would at least come across and kiss her, she yearned, but he went without another word. Her trespasses might be forgiven to a certain extent; forgotten they quite definitely were not.

Wearing another of the new dresses, this time a semifitted shift obliquely striped in varying tones of cream and beige, she went through to the living room to find both father and son awaiting her.

''I helped Chelsea to choose her new clothing,'' claimed Dimitris with pride. ''We visited many stores!''

''All in the space of a couple of hours after lunch,'' Chelsea hastened to add, not wanting it to be taken that they'd spent every minute going round the shops.

''An excellent choice on both accounts,'' Nikos approved. ''We must make sure our programme today befits such a garment.''

with a brief *"efcharisto"* to whatever message was finally relayed.

"The marriage is to take place tomorrow," he said. "At present, they can be found at a taverna in the Patission district."

"You're going to stop it." Chelsea made it a statement not a question, her tone flat.

"Certainly I'm going to stop it," he returned hardily. "If the marriage is to take place at all, it must be in the proper manner."

Her head jerked up, her eyes widening as she searched his face for confirmation that she wasn't misreading anything. "Do you mean you'll help them?"

"I'll speak with Thanassis. There's no certainty of his agreement."

"If the marriage has your backing, I'm sure he'll come round." She hesitated before asking, "What made you change your mind?"

He regarded her impassively. "I didn't say I'd changed my mind. I still believe the man Elini's father chose for her would make her a far better husband than my work-shy cousin."

"But it's Dion she loves," Chelsea said softly. "When you love someone, it's warts and all." She gave him no chance to ridicule that bit of homespun philosophy. "If you're through with me now, I'll get going."

Nikos looked suddenly weary. "I need you to stay with Dimitris while I go and find this taverna."

"How long is that likely to take?"

"An hour—two hours—how can I say?" He paused, expression firming again. "I'll be back as soon as I possibly can."

He'd been gone several minutes before Chelsea stirred herself to get up from the chair. She could at least get her stuff packed in readiness—what there was of it. The rest back on Skalos could stay there.

It was only on reaching the bedroom that she thought about her passport. She hadn't bothered to bring it with her because she hadn't expected to need it, but she certainly wasn't going to get far without it.

Short of going back to fetch it, the only way round the problem was to go to the British Embassy here and report it lost. How long it might take to get a replacement she had no idea. Right now she didn't much care.

Dimitris appeared in the bedroom doorway as she finished packing. "Are we not to go to Delphi?" he asked, looking downcast.

"Not today, I'm afraid," Chelsea confirmed, not sure how to tell him what he had to be told. "I have to go home," she said, trying not to sound too despondent about it. "My own home in England."

Dismay clouded the small fine features. "Why must you go?"

She conjured a smile. "Because I'm needed."

"I don't want you to go!" It was a cry from the heart, his lower lip quivering. "Who will take care of me?"

Chelsea felt her own lip quiver. She went and scooped the boy up in her arms, sitting down on the nearby chair to hug him to her. "Your papa will find someone really nice, you'll see. No more Ledras!"

"I want *you* to stay with me!" Tears were spilling down his cheeks, wetting the front of her dress. "Please, Chelsea!"

"I can't." She kissed the curly head, on the verge of tears herself. "I wish I could, but I just can't."

He made no further spoken plea, just wound his arms about her neck as if to hold her by force, sobbing his heart out. Chelsea didn't attempt to disengage him; it was all she could do to stop herself from howling along with him. It would have come to this anyway in the end, she told herself, rocking the child back and forth in an instinctive comforting motion. Better now than later, when the bond would have grown even deeper. Children had short memories. Dimitris would soon forget her. A great deal more easily than she was going to forget, for certain.

Worn out, he eventually fell asleep. Chelsea eased limbs grown stiff and carried him through to lay him gently down on his bed. It was still only just gone nine-thirty, she realised with a sense of shock, catching a glimpse of her watch as she drew a single sheet over the little figure.

Dimitris still hadn't surfaced when Nikos returned some time after eleven. He looked, Chelsea thought, almost as dispirited as she felt.

"How did it go?" she asked. "Assuming you found them, that is?"

"I found them," he said. "They took a great deal of persuading, but they agreed in the end to allow me to speak with Thanassis on their behalf. A little late in the day, I fear," he added drily, "but all the more reason for the marriage to take place."

"All's well that ends well," Chelsea quoted with deliberated flippancy. "I'm packed and ready, so I'll be out of your hair in a shake of a dog's tail!"

"*Ochi!*" Dimitris came shooting across the room to attach himself to her leg like a limpet. The dark eyes looked huge in the small face lifted to her, but they were filled with determination this time, not tears. "*Ochi,*" he repeated.

Chelsea looked down at him helplessly, then across at Nikos, who was looking on with indefinable expression, lifting her shoulders in a wry little shrug. "I suppose you're going to think I put him up to this too?"

"No," he returned levelly. "Dion told me he was the one who instructed Dimitris to tell no one of the meeting, because you refused to do it. Why did you allow me to believe otherwise?"

"You didn't give me much of an opportunity to deny it," she said. "Not that there seemed a great deal of point anyway. If I was going to be hanged, it might just as well have been for a sheep as for a lamb."

Nikos let out an explosive expletive—at least that was what she took it to be. "If I hear one more of these sayings of yours…!"

Chelsea had put her hands over Dimitris's ears, keeping up the act to the bitter end. "Not in front of the child, please!"

"I want to hear what you're saying," declared the child in question, shaking himself free of her grasp without letting go of her leg. "Tell her she has to stay with us!" he commanded his father, springing a glint of surprised amusement in the latter's eyes.

"The decision must rest with Chelsea herself," he said. "Perhaps she may not wish to stay." He raised his gaze to her face, lifting a questioning eyebrow. "*Do* you?"

She looked back at him in confusion. "You're the one who—" She broke off, mindful of the listening ears below and reluctant to introduce the idea that his father was responsible for her departure.

"I need to speak with Chelsea on her own again," Nikos advised. "I promise you she'll still be here when you return."

Dimitris eyed him for a solemn moment, then slowly released his grip on Chelsea's leg. "You will call me when you finish speaking together?"

"The very moment," Nikos confirmed.

Chelsea bent and rubbed her lower thigh, where the

boy's fierce grip had left imprints in her flesh, struggling to maintain her composure, such as it was.

"You shouldn't make promises you can't be sure of keeping," she murmured.

"I never do that," came the assured rejoinder. "You were saying?"

Chelsea straightened, shaking her head bemusedly. "I can't remember."

"I think you were about to say that I was the one who told you to go."

She gazed at him with furrowed brow. "Well, didn't you?"

"At no time. I was angry with you, yes, but there was never a moment when I contemplated losing you. You've become a part of my life, *phedi*—a very vital part. Of Dimitris's life too. You must know what you mean to the two of us."

"I know what I mean to Dimitris," she said slowly, trying not to read too much into too little. "He means a great deal to me too. But you..."

"But I?" he prompted as she let the words trail away. "You believe my feelings for you so very different from my son's?" He smiled at the look on her face. "I'm not speaking of the physical aspect. Wonderful as I find it to make love to you, there are other needs just as important."

Chelsea could feel a slow unfurling sensation deep down inside her—a spreading warmth. "Such as?" she whispered.

"An ability to talk together, to laugh together, to spend leisure time enjoying the same things. I've never known a woman I could share all of that with before." He paused, eyes firing as he read the expression in hers. "I love you, *agapi mou*. I want you to be my wife—a mother to Dimitris."

"For a man of action, you're doing an awful lot of talking," she said after a moment. "Not that I'm complaining, of course. I mean, would I dare—?"

She broke off with a laugh as he yanked her into his arms, meeting his lips in heartfelt elation. Just a few short minutes ago she had been halfway out of the door. From that to this seemed unbelievable.

"Why did you wait till now to tell me how you feel?" she demanded when he allowed her to take a breath again. "Have you any idea what I've been going through since last night?"

"Not as much as you deserved," he said with mock severity. "How do you imagine it felt to discover that the woman I love had lied to me?"

"Lousy," she conceded. "But I probably wouldn't be here at all if I'd told you the truth to start with."

Nikos smiled. "Yes, you would. I'd have refused you the interview, yes, but it wouldn't have stopped me from wanting you." He ran his fingers through her hair, tilting her face so that he could look into her eyes. "That doesn't mean that I'm prepared to overlook every transgression on your part, so be warned. Greek wives treat their men with respect."

"But I'm not Greek," Chelsea pointed out, tongue-in-cheek. "Surely that gives me a little extra leeway?"

He laughed, shaking his head. "I think I may be—how do you say it—making a shaft for my own back?"

"Rod," she corrected. "Anyway, imagine how boring it would be to have a yes-woman around the whole time. You need stimulation, not tedium."

Nikos caught the hand she was running along his thigh. "I'll remind you of that later. Right now, we have to go and tell Dimitris he is to have a mama, like other boys."

"Maybe even some brothers and sisters too, in time,"

she said happily. "I'd better let them know back home too. Mum's going to throw a fit! Figure of speech," she added blandly, hearing the sigh. "I'll have to teach you a few to toss around the boardroom. Make one hell of an impression on the underlings!"

"I'll make one hell of an impression on you if you don't behave yourself!" Nikos growled, but the laughter wasn't far away. It wouldn't, Chelsea was determined, ever be far away.

The world's bestselling romance series.

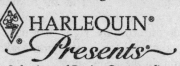

HARLEQUIN®
Presents

Seduction and Passion Guaranteed!

Introducing Jane Porter's exciting new series

THE *Galván Brides*

**The Galván men: proud Argentine aristocrats...
who've chosen American rebels as their brides!**

IN DANTE'S DEBT
Harlequin Presents #2298

Count Dante Galván was ruthless—and though it broke Daisy's heart she had no alternative but to hand over control of her family's stud farm to him. She was in Dante's debt up to her ears! Daisy knew she was far too ordinary ever to become the count's wife— but could she resist his demands that she repay her dues in his bed?

On sale January 2003

LAZARO'S REVENGE
Harlequin Presents #2304

Lazaro Herrera has vowed revenge on Dante, his half brother, who refuses to acknowledge his existence. When Dante's sister-in-law Zoe arrives in Argentina, it seems the perfect opportunity. But the clash of Zoe's blond and blue-eyed beauty with his own smoldering dark looks creates a sexual force so strong that Lazaro's plan begins to fall apart....

On sale February 2003

Pick up a Harlequin Presents® novel and you will enter a world of spine-tingling passion and provocative, tantalizing romance!

Available wherever Harlequin books are sold.

HARLEQUIN®
Makes any time special ®

**Harlequin is proud to have published
more than 75 novels by**

Emma Darcy

Award-
winning Australian
author **Emma Darcy** is a
unique voice in Harlequin
Presents®. Her compelling, sexy,
intensely emotional novels have
gripped the imagination of readers
around the globe, and she's sold
nearly 60 million books
worldwide.

Praise for Emma Darcy:

"Emma Darcy delivers a spicy love story...a fiery conflict
and a hot sensuality."

"Emma Darcy creates a strong emotional premise
and a sizzling sensuality."

"Emma Darcy pulls no punches."

"With exciting scenes, vibrant characters and a layered story line,
Emma Darcy dishes up a spicy reading experience."

—*Romantic Times Magazine*

**Look out for more thrilling stories by Emma Darcy,
coming soon in**

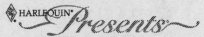